Elsie floated above the snow, deathly pale and not quite solid. Her bare feet grazed the snow's surface but left no tracks. I wanted to turn my head away, but I couldn't help looking at her. I saw her crooked teeth, longer and more yellow than I remembered. Her skin was stretched tight over her skull, and her eyes gleamed in their sockets. She looked like she wanted to take my life and make it hers.

"One crow for sorrow," Elsie whispered in a voice as harsh as the wind on a winter night. "*Your* sorrow."

I finally found my voice. "You're not real, you can't be, you're dead, I saw you in your coffin. I saw them take you away in a hearse. They *buried* you."

ONE FOR SORROW

ONE FOR SORROW

A Ghost Story

MARY DOWNING HAHN

HOUGHTON MIFFLIN HARCOURT
BOSTON   NEW YORK

For information about permission to reproduce selections from this book, write to trade.permissions@hmco.com or to Permissions, Houghton Mifflin Harcourt Publishing Company, 3 Park Avenue, 19th Floor, New York, New York 10016.

hmhco.com

The text was set in 11 pt. Horley Old Style MT Std.

The Library of Congress has cataloged the hardcover edition as follows:
Names: Hahn, Mary Downing, author.
Title: One for sorrow : a ghost story / Mary Downing Hahn.
Description: Boston ; New York : Clarion Books, Houghton Mifflin Harcourt,
[2017] | Summary: "When unlikeable Elsie dies in the influenza pandemic of
1918, she comes back to haunt Annie to make sure she'll be Annie's
best—and only—friend soon"— Provided by publisher.
Identifiers: LCCN 2016010761 | ISBN 9780544818095 (hardcover)
Subjects: | CYAC: Best friends—Fiction. | Friendship—Fiction. |
Ghosts—Fiction. | Influenza Epidemic, 1918-1919—Fiction. | World War,
1914-1918—United States—Fiction. | Horror stories.
Classification: LCC PZ7.H1256 On 2017 | DDC [Fic]—dc23
LC record available at https://lccn.loc.gov/2016010761

ISBN: 978-0-544-81809-5 hardcover
ISBN: 978-1-328-49798-7 paperback

Printed in the United States of America
DOC 10 9 8 7 6 5 4 3 2 1

4500714049

ONE

ALTHOUGH I DIDN'T REALIZE IT, my troubles began when we moved to Portman Street, and I became a student in the Pearce Academy for Girls, the finest school in the town of Mount Pleasant, according to Father. I was shy, maybe even a little timid, and I had no idea how to make friends. In my old town, there were three girls my age living in my neighborhood, and I didn't remember making friends with them. We lived on the same street, and we were friends. It was as simple as that.

But no girls lived on my new street, so when I walked into class on a sunny September day, I didn't know anyone. All I saw was a sea of white blouses, blue ties, and blue skirts. Row after row of them. I was too nervous to notice the faces, just the uniforms.

Miss Harrison introduced me. "Girls, it's my pleasure to introduce Annie Browne, new to our school from the Fairfield Academy in Mount Holly. Please make her feel welcome in true Pearce fashion."

I didn't smile for fear no one would smile back. With my head down, I took my seat, folded my hands on my desktop, and stared at the stack of books Miss Harrison gave me. *World Geography,* the biggest and thickest, was on the bottom. Weighing it down were five more books — *Sixth-Grade Arithmetic, Adventures in Reading Book II, Grammar Handbook, United States History,* and *A Girl's Treasury of Poetry,* as well as a penmanship workbook.

Miss Harrison began the morning exercises with the Lord's Prayer, but before we began the Pledge of Allegiance, she said, "Let us say a prayer for our boys overseas. May God bring them home safely from this terrible war."

We bowed our heads, and I prayed especially hard for Uncle Paul, Mother's brother who was in France fighting the Germans. The newspapers were full of dreadful stories of trenches and poison gas and bombs and battles. I worried every day about my uncle. I wished President Wilson had never declared war, but Father said it was our duty to save Europe from Germany. I was glad he was too old to be drafted.

After we pledged allegiance to the flag, we took our

seats and Miss Harrison pulled down a large map of the world and quizzed us about the war. Tapping her pointer on northeast France, she asked what was happening there. I wasn't sure, so I lowered my head and prayed she wouldn't call on me.

Plenty of hands shot into the air. Miss Harrison looked around the room and said, "Rosie O'Malley. Stand up and tell us what you know."

A red-haired girl in the back row got to her feet. She had so many freckles you could hardly see her skin.

She grinned at the girl who sat beside her. "That's the Argonne Forest," she told Miss Harrison. "We're fighting a big battle there against the dirty rotten Huns."

Miss Harrison frowned. "Correct on location, Rosie, but I've told you before not to use slang. In this class, we speak formal English. Please repeat your answer, using appropriate terminology."

Rosie shrugged. "All right. We're fighting the dirty Germans in the Argonne Forest, and I hope we kill every one of them."

A low giggle spread through the room, and Miss Harrison frowned again. "Just answer, Rosie, without the adjective and your opinions."

Rosie's face turned as red as her hair. "We're fighting the *Germans* in the Argonne Forest, but we all know they're dirty Huns. That's what everybody calls them. Huns, Krauts, Fritz, swine — why can't we say what they are?"

"You may use crude language when you are not in school, Rosie, but in this room you will speak formally. Please see me after school."

Rolling up the map with a snap, Miss Harrison told us to open our arithmetic books. Instead of giggles, I heard soft moans. Whether it was sympathy for Rosie or dread of arithmetic, I couldn't tell. Maybe both.

After a lesson on changing fractions to percentages, we diagrammed long complex sentences that used up a whole page in my notebook and took a spelling test. Not too hard; I only missed two words out of twenty — a solid B. Father would ask why I missed two, of course, but Mother would say there was nothing wrong with a B.

When Miss Harrison dismissed us for recess, I was happy to stretch my legs but worried about going outside to play with girls I didn't know. I walked to the cloakroom slowly, hoping the others had already gotten their coats and rushed to the playground.

Only one girl remained. She had a pale, round face, and her blond hair was pulled tightly into French braids. She was taller than I was and heavier, not actually fat, but definitely not thin. When I reached for my sweater, she smiled at me, revealing a mouthful of the most crooked teeth I'd ever seen.

"My name is Elsie Schneider," she said. "And we're going to be friends, Annie Browne. I knew it when I saw you come through the door."

She grabbed my hand. Her skin was cold and damp, and I wanted to snatch my hand away and wipe it on my skirt. But that would have been rude, so I let her hold it.

Elsie led me down the empty hall. "There's lots you need to know about this school," she said. "Things I wish somebody had told me when I started here last year."

"It seems nice," I said. "As far as schools go," I added so she wouldn't think I was a goody-goody.

"Nice?" Elsie laughed. "Just wait. You'll see. The girls here are all conceited snobs. They've already chosen who they want for friends. They didn't choose me, and they won't choose you, either."

She squeezed my hand so hard it hurt and added, "But that's all right because we have each other."

Pushing open a door, she stopped on the top step. Below us, the girls in our class played tag, jumped rope, and gathered in laughing groups.

Of all the girls, Rosie laughed the loudest and talked the most. She was like a toy wound up too tight. She swung high and ran fast, and everyone followed her, doing what she did, and calling "Rosie, wait." "Rosie, I'll share my cookies with you if you sit next to me at lunch." "No, sit next to me, and I'll give you my cupcake, devil's food with chocolate icing." "Rosie, come to the sweet shop after school, and I'll buy you a peppermint stick."

Rosie never said yes or no. She laughed and kept going as if she was waiting for the best offer.

Elsie made a face. "And that girl, Rosie O'Malley, is the worst one of all. You saw how rude she was to Miss Harrison. She's absolutely awful. I hate her. Don't you?"

"I don't even know her." In my eyes, Rosie was exciting, a girl who did things and had lots of friends. She was much more interesting than Elsie, but I certainly wasn't ready to say that and risk losing the only friend I'd made so far.

"Do you want to play hopscotch or swing or anything?" I asked Elsie. It seemed to me some of the girls had noticed us standing apart. A few whispered among themselves, looked at Elsie and me, and laughed. I didn't like being stared at. I checked to see if my sweater was buttoned crooked. Maybe a shoelace was untied. Maybe my hair had a tangle Mother hadn't seen or I had jam on my mouth.

In answer to my question, Elsie shook her head. "All the swings are taken. And I hate hopscotch, don't you?

It's almost as stupid as jump rope and jacks. Baby stuff, *I* think."

"Hopscotch is okay. You know, if there's nothing else to do." Here I was again, trying not to offend her. Why couldn't I speak up and say I loved hopscotch? Like jump rope and jacks, I was good at it. My friends at my old school called me the hopscotch queen.

Elsie took my hand again. "Let's walk together, Annie."

Conscious of being watched, I let her hold my hand and lead me down the steps. A group of girls thronged around us. Rosie grabbed Elsie's and my linked hands and held them up to show everyone.

"Look," she shouted. "Fat Elsie has a girlfriend!"

I snatched my hand away, but Rosie and everyone else laughed. One of Rosie's friends gave Elsie a little shove and looked at Rosie to see if she was impressed.

"Better not make Fat Elsie mad," Rosie sneered. "She'll tell Miss Harrison."

Someone began a chant, and the others took it up.

Tattletale
ate a snail,
threw it up in the garbage pail.

Elsie pulled me away. "Come on, Annie. Those girls aren't worth a wooden nickel. Who cares what they say? Not me."

Trying to ignore the other girls, I walked away with Elsie. Whether or not she cared, *I* cared.

Elsie pulled me closer. "I hate Rosie so much," she hissed in my ear. "Someday I'll get even with her. Just wait. You'll see."

Behind us, the other girls chanted our names and laughed. "Elsie and Annie sitting in a tree, fat and ugly as they can be."

When the bell rang, I was more than ready to join the line waiting to go back to our classroom. On my first day at Pearce, I'd made one friend and twenty enemies.

Elsie and I took a place at the back of the line. Ahead of us, the other girls giggled and jostled one another until Miss Harrison pulled a whistle out of her coat pocket and blew a warning blast.

Immediately the line straightened and everyone stopped giggling. Two by two, we walked quietly inside and took our seats without a sound. Everyone, that is, except Elsie. She stopped at Miss Harrison's desk and whispered a few words. Miss Harrison picked up her pencil and wrote something down.

"You may take your seat now, Elsie," Miss Harrison said without looking up.

"Yes, ma'am." Shooting a sly look at Rosie, Elsie sashayed to her seat and grinned at me. The dirty looks directed to Elsie shifted to me. The other girls were holding me to blame for whatever Elsie told Miss Harrison.

"Tattletale, ate a snail," someone whispered behind me. My face burned with shame. I'd never tattled on anyone, not once in my whole life. I'd rather have had my tongue torn out than tell. It wasn't fair to lump me with Elsie. Those girls didn't even know me.

"Before we open our readers," Miss Harrison said, "I must tell you that I expect you to exhibit the same good behavior on the playground as you do in the classroom. I will not tolerate name calling or teasing."

What had Elsie told Miss Harrison? Out of the corner of my eye, I saw Rosie make a face at Elsie, carefully shielding herself from Miss Harrison's watchful eye. Someone giggled. Miss Harrison looked at Rosie, who sat with her hands folded primly on her desk.

The rest of the day passed slowly. When the dismissal bell finally rang, my first thought was to escape from Elsie, but she was by my side before I had buttoned my sweater.

As we left the classroom, Elsie paused in the doorway

to take a quick look at Rosie, who was standing at the black-board, her back to us, writing, *I will use proper language in school.* Her handwriting sloped upward and her letters were poorly formed, but maybe that was because she was in a hurry to finish.

"I hope Miss Harrison makes her write it five hundred times," Elsie whispered.

Miss Harrison had ears as sharp as her eyes. She gave Elsie and me an angry look, clearly warning us we'd be writing on the blackboard ourselves if we didn't leave at once. Rosie turned her head and made a face at us both.

Once more, I was being blamed along with Elsie for things I hadn't done.

As we walked down the school steps — it was against the rules to run, according to Elsie — she said, "You know what I think?"

I shook my head.

"Miss Harrison should make Rosie write it five *thousand* times and then erase it and tell her to start all over again, using her best handwriting instead of that scribble scrabble she's doing."

Elsie smiled with so much glee I turned my head away. How was I to escape from her?

TWO

WHEN WE REACHED PORTMAN STREET, I said, "I live just around the corner." Thinking I was rid of her at last, I started walking toward home, but to my disappointment, Elsie turned the corner with me.

"Do you live near here?" I crossed my fingers behind my back and hoped she'd say no.

"I live way across town, in the opposite direction." She took my hand. "I thought we'd go to your house and play."

I tried to think of a reason she couldn't come home with me, but my mind was numb. So hand in hand, we walked up the front steps and went inside.

Mother was sitting on the couch reading a magazine. When she saw me, she smiled and got to her feet to give me a hug and a kiss. "How was school, darling?"

Before I could answer, Elsie said, "This awful girl named Rosie was mean to Annie. And the other girls ganged up on us. But Annie and I are best friends, and we don't care what they say or do. We have each other."

Mother looked at Elsie as if she hadn't actually noticed her until she spoke up.

"This is Elsie Schneider," I told her. "She's in my class."

Mother smiled at Elsie but immediately looked at me. With concern, she asked, "Whatever happened, Annie? You had plenty of friends in our old neighborhood."

"Oh, but Mrs. Browne, you don't know the girls at Pearce," Elsie butted in again. "They're mean and conceited, and they do everything Rosie says. They like who *she* likes and hate everybody else."

Mother turned to me. "Should I speak to Miss Harrison about this?"

"No," I said, "please don't. You'll just make it worse."

"They already think we're tattletales," Elsie put in.

"I was about to fix hot chocolate." Mother spoke as if a treat might make Elsie and me feel better. "Would you two like some?"

"Oh, yes," Elsie said. "Do you have cookies? I *love* vanilla wafers."

We followed Mother to the kitchen. "You have such a

pretty house," Elsie told Mother. "It's so comfortable and cozy."

"Why, thank you." Mother smiled at Elsie. "Aren't you sweet?"

Elsie glanced at me, obviously pleased that Mother liked her.

Mother warmed milk and melted chocolate in the double boiler. Elsie watched her add sugar and butter.

As soon as Mother set steaming mugs and a plate of vanilla wafers on the table, Elsie reached for a cookie and stuffed it into her mouth as if she thought someone might slap her hand. She burned her tongue because she gulped a mouthful of hot chocolate before it cooled enough to drink. I noticed Mother watching Elsie as if she was wondering whether all the girls at Pearce behaved this way. If so, perhaps someone should teach them table manners.

"Elsie," Mother said, "if you eat too many cookies, you won't have room for dinner."

Elsie merely shrugged and took another cookie. With her mouth full, she said, "I warned you I love vanilla wafers."

When not a crumb remained and all the hot chocolate was gone, Elsie asked if we could play in my room for a while.

As she followed me upstairs, she caressed the oak

banister. "I love the way this wood feels," she said. "It's so smooth. No splinters or chipped paint like my house."

I didn't know what she expected me to say, so I pretended I hadn't heard her.

At the door to my room, Elsie stopped and stared. "This is all yours? Everything in it? Oh, Annie, you are so lucky!"

Something in her voice made me feel ashamed. Did I have too much? I'd never thought about it before. My friends in my old neighborhood had rooms like mine, filled with toys and books. I guess I'd thought everyone did.

Elsie ran around my room, taking in every detail. She studied each room in my dollhouse. Mother and I had furnished it like a Victorian mansion. A family of china dolls lived in it, along with several servants.

"I wish I lived in a house just like this!" she exclaimed. "Fancy furniture, pretty wallpaper, velvet curtains." As she spoke, she touched the tiny sofas and chairs and examined the miniature plates on the table. She picked up each doll and studied its clothing.

From the dollhouse, she moved to shelves of books, touching them on their spines as if she were taking inventory. She tried out the rocking chair Father had made for me when I was little. She picked up the dolls sitting on a shelf and examined each one. She looked out my window at our big backyard, sloping away to a line of trees. She studied the floral design on the wallpaper. She even opened the doors of the tall walnut wardrobe in the corner and flipped through my skirts and dresses and blouses.

Finally she sat down on my bed and gave a little bounce as if she was testing the mattress. "You are my best friend in the whole world," she said. "What good times we'll have playing here."

I tried to smile, but my face felt as rigid as the oak banister she'd admired. She didn't notice my silence. She picked up Edward Bear and squeezed his tummy to make him growl.

"What makes that noise?" She poked Edward's belly harder. "We should cut him open and find out."

I tried to snatch Edward away from her, but she moved out of my reach. "Give him to me," I cried. "I've had him since I was a baby. I'd never ever hurt him."

"That's stupid. How can you hurt a toy? He's just a stuffed animal with half his fur gone and one eye missing. Old and ugly and smelly."

In disgust, she tossed Edward aside and grabbed Antoinette, my favorite doll. She laid her on her back and watched her eyes close. She sat her up and watched them open. Then she tipped her back and forth to hear her say "Mama."

It sounded as if poor Antoinette were crying out for me to rescue her, but when I reached for her, Elsie hugged the doll. "Let me hold her for a while. You have so many dolls, and I don't have any. Not even one."

"Mama, Mama," cried Antoinette.

I didn't like the rough way Elsie handled Antoinette, but I let her hold her. It wouldn't do to be selfish. "Be careful with her," I whispered. "She's fragile."

"Don't worry. I won't hurt her." Elsie hugged her tighter. "Mama," cried the doll.

When was Elsie going home? She'd been here a long time. It was almost dark. I decided to give her a hint. "It's nearly dinnertime," I said. "Won't your mother be worried about you?"

"Oh no, I can stay as long as I want." She smiled at me. "Nobody cares where I am or when I come home. In fact they'd be happy if they never saw me again."

I stared at her, shocked. "You don't mean that, Elsie. Of course your parents care where you are."

"Not everyone is as lucky as you, Annie." Elsie's voice rose. "Do you think *I* get hot chocolate and cookies when I come home from school? Do you think *I* have a room full of toys and books? Or a wardrobe of pretty dresses?"

Not knowing what to say, I bent my head and smoothed the pleats in my skirt. How could I know what Elsie had or didn't have? I'd never even been to her house — and if I had my way, I'd never go there or invite her here again.

Elsie leaned so close I felt her breath on my face. "I'd give anything to have a mother like yours. It's not fair that you have so much and I have nothing!"

"But your mother —"

"You stupid goose, I don't have a mother!"

"Everybody has a mother —"

"Not me," Elsie yelled so loud spit came out of her mouth and hit me in the face. "My mother, my *real* mother, died when I was born. I never even saw her."

I wanted to feel sorry for Elsie, I *did* feel sorry for her, but the way she was screaming scared me. If she kept it up, Mother would hear her and come running upstairs.

But she didn't stop. She kept on yelling as if it were my fault I had a mother and she didn't.

"It's not fair Mama died. It's not fair!" Suddenly she lowered her voice to a whisper. "Sometimes I *hate* Mama. If she hadn't died, my father wouldn't have married Hilda."

She sat back and glared at me. "I bet you think I'm horrible, don't you?"

Oh, yes, I thought, *she is horrible.* If only she'd leave, go away, never come back. I didn't want to see her again, I didn't want to be her friend. She'd said it herself — she was *truly* horrible.

Keeping my feelings to myself for fear of making her even angrier, I asked if Hilda was her stepmother.

"What a dumb question," Elsie said. "Didn't I just say my father married her?"

Yes, of course, she had just said that, but she'd called her Hilda instead of Mother, or whatever you call a stepmother, and that confused me.

"Hilda's the kind of stepmother you read about in fairy tales. She hates me, and I hate her. If she dared, she'd leave me in a forest to die like a babe in the wood."

"But what about your father? He must —"

"Papa thinks it's my fault Mama died. I killed her getting born." She looked at me as if daring me to say something. Anything at all. No matter what it was, she'd get mad all over again.

When I didn't say a word, Elsie turned her attention to Antoinette and began undressing her. I watched her pull at buttons and yank at my doll's dress.

"Stop — what are you doing? You'll tear her clothes." I reached for the doll, but Elsie kept me from rescuing her.

"I just want to see what she looks like naked." Before I could stop her, Elsie took off my doll's dress, petticoat, lace-trimmed bloomers, shoes, and stockings.

Her leather body and china limbs on display, poor Antoinette sprawled in Elsie's lap. After examining the way the doll's joints worked, Elsie turned her attention to Antoinette's hair. "Is her wig made of real human hair or horsehair? It feels real — maybe it came from a dead person. Did you ever think of that?"

I shook my head. "I'm sure it didn't," I said, hoping I was right.

"She has a big hole in the top of her head, doesn't she?"

"Yes, it's where the doll maker put in her eyes and her teeth and her tongue." Suddenly I was worried. I reached again for my doll, but Elsie held her tightly.

"It's hidden under her hair, right?" To my horror, Elsie tugged at Antoinette's wig as if she meant to pull it off and examine the hole.

"Don't, you'll ruin her!" This time I grabbed Antoinette's leg and pulled. Her leg came loose in my hand, and Elsie threw the doll at me.

"Selfish, take her!" she cried as Antoinette flew over my head and hit the wall with a shattering sound.

I leapt up and scooped Antoinette into my arms. Her face was cracked, and her eyes had fallen back into her head. "Mama," she cried "Mama."

"It's your fault," Elsie said. "If you hadn't pulled her leg off, I wouldn't have dropped her."

"You didn't drop her, you threw her!"

"Did not."

"Did too!"

Just then Mother called us to come downstairs. Leaving poor Antoinette on the bed surrounded by her pretty clothes, I ran down the steps with Elsie right behind me.

"You better not tell," she hissed in my ear. "You'll be sorry if you do."

"Elsie," Mother said, "it's dark out. How far away do you live?"

Sniffing the good smells of roast chicken and fresh baked rolls, Elsie said, "Annie invited me to stay for dinner."

Before I could say I'd done no such thing, Mother frowned at me. "Oh, Annie, you should ask before you invite a guest to stay." Turning to Elsie, she said, "I'm sorry, dear, but I don't have enough food for a fourth person. Maybe another time."

Elsie looked sad, but she said. "Oh, that's all right, Mrs. Browne. It's not your fault." Here she gave me a sly look. "I guess I should go. It's a long walk from here. But don't worry about me. I'm not afraid of the dark."

Taking her sweater from the stand in the hall, she prepared to leave, but Mother stopped her. "Wait a minute,

Elsie," she said. "My husband will be here soon. He'll be glad to take you home."

Sure enough, I heard Father's car in the driveway. In a few moments, he opened the front door and stepped inside. He looked at Elsie and then turned to me. "Well, well," he said. "I see you've made a friend already."

Elsie took my hand and squeezed it hard enough to hurt but not enough for anyone but me to notice. "As soon as I saw Annie, I just knew we'd be best friends."

She squeezed my hand again, and I smiled weakly. My parents didn't seem to notice my lack of enthusiasm at Elsie's proclamation.

"Elsie," Mother said. "if you tell Mr. Browne where you live, he'll drive you home."

"You have a *car?*" Elsie looked at Mother as if she'd said Father had a chariot drawn by six white horses. "I've never ridden in a car. Papa says we can't afford it, what with the war and all."

"I'll be happy to give you your first ride," Father said in that gallant way of his.

Elsie clapped her hands. "Can Annie come with us?"

"Of course she can." Neither Mother nor Father thought to ask if I wanted to go. Nor did I say I didn't want to go.

Elsie grabbed my sweater and handed it to me. Coward that I was, I trudged outside behind her and my father. The night was cool, and an autumn wind sent fallen leaves scurrying down the street. I glanced back at the warm light shining out our windows. Why hadn't I spoken up and said I'd stay at home?

THREE

ELSIE INSISTED ON SITTING in the back seat with me so we could talk while Father drove.

"Your parents are so nice," she whispered. "I wish I could live with you. Do you think I could? You wouldn't be an only child, and neither would I. We'd be sisters and share everything."

Before I could stop myself, I said, "Are you crazy? Why would my parents adopt you? You're not an orphan, and even if you were—"

"I knew you'd say that—you don't want to share anything, do you? Not your stupid doll or your ugly teddy bear or anything else. You're a spoiled, selfish girl, and you're lucky to have me for a friend."

She sat back in the seat and stared out the window. For a few moments, she was silent. Then she turned away from the window and slid across the seat to my side. "Living at your house probably wouldn't be any better than living at my house. I'd just have nicer things."

"What do you mean?"

"How do your parents punish you?"

It was a strange question, but I answered anyway. "What all parents do, I guess. Mother scolds me, and Father has a talk with me about what I did and why I did it."

"Liar," Elsie said. "I bet your father whips you with his belt. And then he locks you in the basement and leaves you in the dark to think about it."

I stared at Elsie in disbelief. "My father would *never* do anything like that."

"Well, lucky, lucky you. It's what my papa does." She glared at me as if it were my fault she got beaten and I didn't. "And Hilda doesn't care. She never tries to stop him, even when I'm down on the floor begging and crying."

"You must be making that up," I whispered, shocked that she'd lie about her parents and scared she was telling the truth. "I can't believe your father could be that mean."

"Well, that's why I want to live with you." She grabbed my little finger and bent it back so far I winced in pain. "But if I can't live with you, at least I can play at your house every day and be your best friend."

With that, Elsie leaned over the seat to tap Father's shoulder. "Turn at the next corner. My house is in the middle of the block."

Father drove slowly down a street lined with narrow brick row houses. "Which one, Elsie?"

"This one." She pinched my arm and said, "See you tomorrow, Annie. I can't wait to play with your dollhouse."

I rubbed my arm as I watched Elsie run up a few steps and open her front door. A man's face looked down at her. His arm reached out and yanked her inside. Even from where I sat, I knew her father was angry. What if she'd told the truth? What if her father was whipping her right now?

It was too dreadful to think about. I climbed into the front seat beside Father. He smelled of pipe tobacco and hair cream, a special Father smell I loved. I liked the feel of his tweed overcoat and the way his hands held the steering wheel. Now that Elsie was gone, I felt safe.

"Well, she's an odd little creature," Father said.

"Yes, she is." *Odder than you know,* I thought.

"She must like you very much to walk so far out of her way to see you."

"I guess so." I snuggled closer to him and took a deep

breath of happiness. How lucky I was to have a father who'd never whip me or lock me in a cellar, no matter what I did. Not that I believed Elsie, of course. I already knew she was a liar.

When we were home, I ran up to my room and gathered Antoinette, her leg, and her torn and wrinkled clothing into a bundle. Cradling her in my arms, I wept over her as if she were a dead child, a child I'd killed without meaning to.

"It's my fault," I told her poor cracked face. "I should never have let Elsie hold you."

"Mama," Antoinette said.

I opened her little trunk, the one she'd come in one Christmas, and laid her among her silk dresses and cotton petticoats. Kissing her, I closed the lid and put the trunk in the back of the wardrobe. I didn't want Mother to find her and ask what happened. Somehow Elsie would know if I told Mother the truth. And then she'd make me sorry — she'd said so.

Instead of going downstairs, I sat on my bed and hugged Edward Bear. Why had I thought Elsie and I could be friends? She'd driven the other girls away from me. She'd yelled at me because her mother was dead and mine wasn't. She'd wanted to rip Edward open to see how his growler worked. She'd broken Antoinette. She'd threatened to make me sorry if I told Mother about the doll.

And she'd pinched my arm so hard it still hurt. I rolled up my sleeve and looked at the bruise she'd made.

I hugged Edward tighter. How was I to get away from Elsie?

"Annie," Father called up the steps, "dinner is served."

I kissed Edward and sat him on my bed. It comforted me to think of him waiting there for me.

Slowly I went downstairs. I didn't touch the banister. Elsie had contaminated it with her hand. In fact she'd tainted my room and everything in it.

As Father passed my plate to me, he said, "You were so worried no one at Pearce Academy would like you, but you've made a friend already."

I nodded and began to cut up my chicken, hoping I'd be able to eat at least few mouthfuls.

Mother looked at me. "Your father says Elsie lives on the other side of town. I hope her parents weren't worried about her coming home after dark." She took a sip of water. "If you stayed out that late, I'd probably call the police."

"She didn't seem to think her parents would care," I said.

"I'm sure she was wrong." Mother ate a forkful of mashed potatoes and then said, "She's so different from the girls in our old neighborhood. I can't help wondering why you chose her for a friend."

Father sighed. "Now, Ida, don't be snobbish. You don't even know the girl."

Mother looked cross. "I'm not being snobbish," she said. "Elsie seems neglected, needy . . . Oh, I don't know how to say it. I feel sorry for her."

Father leaned toward me. "Well, Annie, what do you think about your new friend?"

I kept my head down and poked at my lima beans, a vegetable I truly hated. What was there to say about Elsie? That she'd broken my favorite doll? That she insisted on being my friend? That none of the girls at school liked her? That I didn't like her?

"She wanted to be my friend," I said at last. "No one else did."

"Well," Father said, "this was just the first day, Annie. Mark my words, once the others get to know you, you'll have so many friends you won't know what to do with them all."

Ha, I thought, *how will they get to know me with Elsie clinging to me like a leech?*

The subject changed to Pearce Academy. Did I like my teacher? *Too soon to tell,* I thought, but I told my parents she seemed nice. "She's not old and cranky like Miss Porter at Fairfield School. She's strict, though."

Mother asked if the curriculum was about right for me,

neither too hard nor too easy. Again, it was too early to tell, but I said it was fine. "We had a spelling test, and I only had two wrong out of ten — a B."

Just as I knew he would, Father raised his eyebrows and said I could do better.

"Do you think you'll be happy at Pearce?" Mother asked.

If I can get rid of Elsie, I thought, but to them I said, "It's no better or worse than any other school, I imagine."

That seemed to be the end of their questions. Mother served apple pie and poured coffee for Father. Although I loved apple pie, I took a few bites and pushed it away.

Father looked at me. "You haven't eaten much tonight, Annie."

"It's my fault," Mother said. "I let the girls stuff themselves with cookies and cocoa. You'd think Elsie had never had such a treat in her life. I suspect she's not eating her dinner either."

After we cleared table, Mother and I washed and dried the dishes and then joined Father in the parlor. Even though it wasn't really cold enough yet, Father lit a fire. I cuddled on the sofa beside Mother. Father took a seat in his armchair and opened the evening paper. The fire popped and snapped. The room was cozy and warm.

For the first time since Elsie had left, I felt safe. She was gone. Maybe she wouldn't come back. Maybe I'd make new friends tomorrow.

I opened *Anne of Green Gables*, a book I'd already read more than once, and thought of redheaded Rosie dashing around the playground. She had a sparkle that reminded me of Anne, a promise of mischief and fun and jokes and secrets. If only I could be *her* friend.

Father looked up from the paper. "According to the *New York Times*, we're slowly making progress against the Germans. If all goes well, the war might be over before Christmas."

Mother sighed and laid down her knitting. "It would be wonderful to have Paul home for the holidays. I worry about him constantly. The trenches, the nerve gas, the disease." She shuddered as if her words had brought the war into our cozy parlor. "So much suffering and pain and death. I wish this country had stayed out of the war."

"We've talked about this before," Father said. "We should have gone in when the Germans sank the *Lusitania*. The war would probably be over now if the president hadn't been such a pacifist."

"Wilson was wise to delay," Mother said. "Even more of our boys would be dead if he'd declared war sooner."

While my parents argued quietly, I worried about Uncle Paul. What if his name appeared on one of the lists of casualties posted every day in the newspaper? What if he never came home? Or what if he came home — but without his legs? What if he came home with "battle fatigue"? He could be a mental case from the gas the Germans used. I'd seen pictures in the paper. I knew how awful the war was.

I snuggled against Mother's side, comforted by her warmth. If only I could end the war with one big powerful wish and bring Uncle Paul back. And all the other Yanks as well.

As Rosie said, the Germans were dirty rotten Huns, and I hated them. Everyone did. Even Miss Harrison. If I ever met a German, I'd spit in his face.

FOUR

THE NEXT MORNING, Elsie was waiting for me at the school gate. As soon as she saw me, she pushed through the crowd of girls entering the schoolyard and ran across the street to meet me. "Were your parents angry about the doll?"

"I didn't tell them."

"I knew you wouldn't tattle." Elsie seized my hand and swung it as we crossed the street. "Your parents must be rich — all the things you have and the big house you live in. I'm so glad we're friends."

While the other students pushed past us, laughing and talking, Elsie pulled me aside. "I got in trouble for coming home late. Papa whipped me, and Hilda sent me to bed with no supper. But that's not the worst of it.'"

She tightened her grip on my hand, and we walked up the school steps together. The other girls were all inside, and she paused at the door to look me in the eye.

"As part of my punishment, Papa says I can't go anywhere for a week. That means you and I won't be able to play at your house till next Monday."

"Oh, that's too bad." I tried to sound truly disappointed, but not very deep inside, I was so happy I could have danced into our classroom.

Elsie's eyes narrowed with suspicion. "Maybe you're glad you won't have to share your toys with me," she said in a low, whiny voice. "Maybe you don't want to be best friends after all."

With a scowl on her face, she shoved the heavy school door open, darted inside, and let the door slam in my face.

I stood where I was for a moment, stunned. What kind of a friend was Elsie? She'd ruined my doll, she'd slammed a heavy door in my face. What would she do next?

The bell rang as I tugged the door open. In all my years at Fairfield, I'd never been late. This was only my second day at Pearce, and I was tardy. It seemed nothing was going well for me at my new school.

Alone and afraid, I walked down the empty hallway. By the time I reached my door, I saw the girls standing for the Lord's Prayer. Ignoring their turned heads and watchful eyes, I tiptoed into the cloakroom to hang up my coat.

"Girls," Miss Harrison said, "we shall wait until Annie Browne deigns to join us for the Lord's Prayer."

Humiliated, I slunk to my desk and stood beside it, so flustered I barely remembered the words of the prayer.

After we pledged our allegiance to the flag and prayed for the soldiers, Miss Harrison beckoned to me. Aware of the eyes tracking me, I walked to her big oak desk and waited with my head down.

"Do you have an excuse for being tardy, Annie?"

I felt Elsie staring at my back, her eyes like drills, daring me to say she'd slammed the door. "No, ma'am."

"I'll forgive you this time. After all, it's your second day with us, and you were only a few minutes late." She hesitated. "But I'll keep you in for recess today."

"Yes, ma'am, I'm sorry, ma'am. It won't happen again." I returned to my seat. It may sound strange, but I was happy to miss recess. I hadn't enjoyed walking around the playground with Elsie yesterday, and I was sure to enjoy it even less today.

For the rest of the week, I dreaded recess. Because my classmates continued to link me with Elsie, they disliked me. I watched them play onesies and foursquare, I watched them jump rope, I watched them chase one another and swing and seesaw — all things I loved to do, but Elsie kept my hand in hers and never gave me a chance to approach them.

"You're my best friend." She squeezed my hand so hard I winced. "You and me, best friends forever."

Rosie ran past us laughing. Lucy and Eunice chased her, but she outran them both. Grabbing an empty swing, she stood on the seat and pumped herself higher and higher. It looked as if she'd go right over the top.

Eunice took a swing from another girl and tried to go higher than Rosie, but she never got close.

Elsie gave me a hard nudge with her elbow. "Why are you watching that stupid showoff?"

Rosie chose that moment to launch herself out of the swing into the air. She landed in the dirt but got up laughing. She'd ripped the knees of her stockings. "Dare you to jump!" she yelled at Eunice.

Eunice let the swing slow before she jumped. Even so, she sat down when she landed.

"I hate them both," Elsie muttered. "Especially Rosie. I wish she'd broken her leg. It would've served her right, don't you agree, Annie?"

I shrugged. Elsie took my hand and led me away from

the swings. "Girls shouldn't do things like that. They could hurt their insides."

I wasn't sure what Elsie meant, but I hoped she was wrong. I'd been jumping out of swings for years, and as far as I knew, my insides were fine.

On Monday, the very day she'd be allowed to visit me, Elsie didn't come to school. When I noticed her empty seat, my heart flipped. I held my breath while Miss Harrison called roll. If Elsie didn't show up soon, I was free to be on my own at recess. The thought scared me dizzy. Without my hand in Elsie's and her mouth against my ear whispering things about them, would the girls see me differently?

At recess time, I delayed going to the cloakroom by sharpening my pencils, all five of them, even the ones that didn't need it. By the time I made my appearance on the playground, everyone was swinging or seesawing or gathered in groups whispering secrets and laughing. Sure they were talking about me, I joined the crowd gathered around Rosie. She was bouncing a red rubber ball, and the girls were chanting, "Seven, eight, nine O'Leario, ten, eleven, twelve O'Leario." With every bounce, Rosie swung her leg over the ball, caught it, and bounced it again.

One, two, three O'Leario was one of my favorite games at Fairfield. In fact, I was playground champion. I itched to take a turn when Rosie missed. Inching forward, I watched her closely. She was good. But no better than I was.

"Sixteen, seventeen, eighteen O'Leario," the girls chanted. Rosie bounced and swung her leg, bounced and swung her leg, but finally on "twenty-seven O'Leario," the sole of her shoe grazed the ball and she missed.

The crowd of girls cheered, and someone started singing, "For she's a jolly good fellow, for she's a jolly good fellow."

With her face flushed and her blouse untucked, Rosie threw her arms up in the air and laughed. "Let's see someone beat that!"

Before I could think about what I was doing, I stepped into the circle surrounding Rosie. "I can."

A soul-killing silence fell. The girls stared at me and then began whispering to one another.

"Where's your twin sister today?" Rosie asked.

I shrugged and looked at the ground. I'd made a mistake. But if I walked away now, they'd never be friends with me.

"Oooh," Eunice said. "Get away from me — you have Elsie's germs."

"Cooties," Lucy shouted, "Annie has cooties just like Fat Elsie."

The girls all backed away, holding their hands over their mouths and noses.

"Oh, let her try." Rosie tossed me the ball. "Let's see how far you get."

I missed the ball because I hadn't expected her to throw it. The girls laughed and drew around Rosie and me in a circle.

"She'll be out after one, two, three," Eunice said.

"Give her a chance," Jane said. Of all of the girls in my class, she was the sweetest. I'd never heard her say a mean word, not even to Elsie. I smiled at her, and she smiled back.

Okay, I said to myself, *I can do this. I'll pretend I'm at Fairfield and these girls are my friends.*

Concentrating hard, I bounced the ball and began. At first I was the only one chanting, but by the time I got to ten, eleven, twelve O'Leario, Jane and a few others had joined me.

The sound of their voices encouraged me, and on I went on. When the count was "nineteen, twenty, twenty-one," everyone was chanting.

The count reached twenty-seven, and still I hadn't missed. On I went, past Rosie, all the way to thirty-three before I failed to catch the ball. I watched it bounce into the crowd and disappear.

For a moment, everyone stared at me in disbelief. If I'd expected them to cheer or sing "For Annie's a jolly good fellow," I'd have been very disappointed.

"I call for a rematch." Eunice picked up the ball and tossed it to Rosie.

Rosie caught it but turned to me with a grin. "Good job, Annie Browne. Maybe we can have a rematch some other time."

"Okay." I smiled at her. Before I could say anything else, the bell rang, and we lined up at the school door.

Jane touched my hand. "You were really good," she said. "I can never get past ten O'Learios. It just plain wears me out to swing my leg over that ball."

"I played it all the time at my old school. It's always been one of my favorite games."

"I like jacks," Jane said. "And pick-up sticks and tiddlywinks, games you sit down to play. I don't get so tired."

"They're fun too."

"How come you never played games at recess before?" Rosie asked.

I hadn't noticed her standing behind me. "On my first

day, Elsie made friends with me. She doesn't like games. But I do."

Rosie looked at me. "Who would you rather be friends with? Elsie or me?"

My face turned red. "You, of course."

We linked pinky fingers and laughed. That's how easy it was to toss Elsie aside and become part of Rosie's gang.

Every day after that, I dreaded Elsie's return to school. I didn't know what she'd do when she saw me running around the playground with Rosie and her gang. Truthfully, I'd been a little scared of her since she'd ruined Antoinette. And the way she talked about her parents and the other girls in our class, even timid ones like Jane who never did anything to her. What would she do to me when she found I'd betrayed her?

The next week, Elsie showed up at the school gate. Her nose was red and running, and she had a balled up hanky in her fist. When she saw me, she began coughing loudly and dramatically.

"Oh, Annie," she said, "I've been so sick. I thought you'd come to see me. I swear I had such a high fever the doctor said I was at death's door. I have a delicate constitution, you know."

Grabbing my hand with the same hand that held the

germy handkerchief, she said, "I've missed you so much, but we can go to your house after school today and play with your dollhouse. That will make me feel so much better. Do you think maybe your mother will fix hot chocolate and give us cookies again?"

While Elsie prattled away, I grew more and more desperate. What was I to do? What was I to say? She thought we were still friends, she thought I wanted her to come to my house and probably destroy my dollhouse, but she was wrong. She was never coming to my house again. Besides, I'd made plans to go to the candy store with Rosie and Jane after school.

And then Rosie was beside me, grinning at Elsie. "Look who's back. I was hoping I'd never see your fat, ugly face again."

Elsie moved closer me. "Leave me alone, Rosie O'Malley. I'm still weak from being sick. If you come any closer, I'll tell Miss Harrison."

"Ooooh, you and your big bad cooties!" Rosie gave Elsie a little push.

Elsie began to cough again. "I'm telling, I'm telling." She grabbed my hand and started pulling me toward the school steps.

"Let go of Annie!" Rosie slapped Elsie's hand. "In case you haven't noticed, she's my friend now."

Elsie stared at me. Her nose was running over her mouth, two thick yellow streams of germs. "That can't be true, Annie."

Without answering, I ran across the street with Rosie. "Charge," Rosie yelled as we dashed up the school steps. "Charge the hill!"

I didn't look back, but I imagined Elsie standing alone on the street, her nose running, watching me, her supposed best friend forever, deserting her.

I thought I'd feel worse than I actually did, but truly it was a relief to be rid of Elsie. No more damp hand holding mine, no more whining and complaining, no more visits to my house. I was free of Elsie forever!

FIVE

I SHOULD HAVE KNOWN that getting away from Elsie wasn't going to be as easy as I hoped.

For a week or two, my former so-called best friend followed me home from school and hung around our front gate. Mother would look outside and see her, sad and pale, swinging forlornly on the gate and watching the house as if waiting for me to come out and play.

"Elsie is out front again, Annie. She was here yesterday and the day before. Have you two quarreled?"

"Not exactly. I just don't like her anymore."

"Well, she seems to like you. Can't you be a little kinder and invite her inside or go out and play with her?"

Why didn't Mother understand? If I went out there, Elsie would *never* go away.

She and Father talked to me about it one night after dinner. It was a chilly evening, and Father lit a fire, but my parents ruined the atmosphere by bringing up Elsie.

"I feel so sorry for her," Mother said. "You'd think you were her only friend."

"I *was* her only friend. I told you no one at school likes her. She lies and cheats and tattles."

Mother and Father looked at each other. "So you dropped Elsie when you made friends with Rosie and Jane?" Father asked.

"You don't understand, Father. I never really liked her. She made me be her friend and then nobody else liked me."

"Are you sure Elsie deserves to be left out?" Mother asked. "She struck me as a sad and lonely girl. It must have hurt her to lose your friendship."

"I'll be right back." I ran upstairs and pulled Antoinette's trunk out of the wardrobe. Lifting my poor, battered doll from her hiding place, I carried her downstairs and laid her in Mother's lap.

"This is what Elsie did to Antoinette." I began to cry at the sight of the doll's ruined face.

"Oh, my goodness." Mother held up the doll for Father to see.

Father shook his head. "I admit I found her a bit odd the night I drove her home. She sat in the back seat whispering to Annie. Secretive, I guess. I'm not surprised to learn she has no friends."

"Oh, Horace," Mother said, "can't you be more compassionate? If you could see her out there, swinging on our gate and gazing at our house as if she's longing to see Annie."

"She does it to make me feel bad," I shouted. "She thinks I'll feel sorry for her and be her friend, but I won't be her friend, no matter what she does!"

Father looked at me. "Annie, don't raise your voice. I won't have it. Please apologize to your mother."

"I'm sorry," I said in a low voice. "I shouldn't have shouted, but you just don't know what Elsie's like. Or how I feel."

Mother shook her head as if she had no more to say about Elsie. Stroking Antoinette's hair, she said, "There's a doll doctor in the city. I'm sure he can make Antoinette look as good as new."

The next day, Rosie and Jane came home with me after school. From the corner, we saw Elsie swinging back and forth on the gate, looking forlorn as usual.

"What's *she* doing at your house?" Rosie looked at me as if she suspected I harbored a secret friendship with Elsie.

"It's not my fault. I didn't invite her," I said. "She

shows up almost every day and waits for me to play with her.
I never do, and after a while she gives up and goes home."

"I'll fix her wagon." Rosie strode down the sidewalk
with Jane at her side, begging her not to be mean.

But sometimes Mean was Rosie's middle name. "Hey,
get off that gate!" she yelled. "You're so fat you'll break it,
and then your Hun father will have to buy a new one for the
Brownes."

Elsie hadn't seen us coming. Rosie startled her so badly
she almost fell off the gate. "My father's not a Hun!"

"Herr Schneider, that's what people call him. They
say he sells horse meat in his butcher shop." Rosie stepped
closer. "Maybe even dog meat. He saves the good stuff for
his German friends."

"That's a lie!"

"Ask my pop, he'll tell you. Everybody but you must
know the truth about your old man."

I glanced at Jane. She looked as surprised as I was.
I'd never heard anything about the butcher shop except
Schneider's high prices. Mother and Father often complained about that, especially when Mother cooked a roast
full of fat and gristle so tough it made my jaws ache to
chew it.

"You better leave me alone," Elsie whined.

Rosie laughed. "Who's going to make me?"

"I'll tell Annie's mother!"

Rosie stood face to face with Elsie, the gate between them. Without warning, Rosie shoved the gate and pushed Elsie back so hard she fell on the sidewalk. As she struggled to get up, she toppled forward and landed on her knees. While we laughed at her clumsiness, Elise examined her torn stockings. "Now I'm really telling!"

"You better not tell *my* mother!" I gave her a push, but not hard enough to knock her down.

Elsie scrambled to her feet. "I hate you, Annie!" She was crying, and her nose was running, and I wished I hadn't shoved her.

But then she spat in my face, and I forgot to feel bad.

"Crybaby," Rosie shouted. "Run home to Mama!"

We watched Elsie go, getting smaller and smaller until she was no more than a distant dot. She had an odd way of running, clumsy, awkward, heavy on her feet, flapping her arms like a bird.

Rosie spit on her palms and rubbed them together. "She won't come back again."

And Rosie was right, at least for the time being.

A few days later, Rosie, Jane, and I were walking home from school. We'd stopped at the corner grocery store to buy dill pickles bigger than hot dogs. Mr. Walker kept them in a barrel and sold them to us wrapped in waxed paper. They were salty and sour and dripping with juice, but Rosie loved them, and so did Jane and I — though not quite as much as Rosie.

Sometimes Jane and I would have preferred to spend our pennies on peppermint sticks or Turkish toffee or licorice, but if Rosie wanted pickles, that's what we got because whatever she liked we liked.

On this particular day, we were talking about Elsie.

"Did you hear what she did to Polly today?" Rosie asked.

"She stole the sandwich right out of her lunch bag," I said. "And ate it at recess. I saw her stuffing it in her mouth like a starving child in Europe. When Miss Harrison asked who did it, everyone looked at Elsie, but she said it wasn't her."

"She's such a liar," Rosie said.

"Maybe she was hungry," Jane said softly. "Sometimes she comes to school without a lunch bag. Haven't you ever noticed?"

Rosie and I looked at each other. I hadn't noticed, and neither had she.

"Yes, but Polly's the smallest girl in our class," Rosie said, "and Elsie's the biggest. She should pick on kids her own size."

"There aren't any kids her size," I said. When Rosie laughed, I felt proud of myself.

"She's a typical Hun." Rosie licked pickle juice from her fingers and threw the wax paper into the gutter. "You know what Pop says about this flu people are getting? It's because of the Germans. They spread the germs. That's why we never buy meat from Herr Schneider. He coughs and sneezes and spits on everything."

"He was born in Germany, did you know that?" Jane asked. "It's why he's got that accent."

"Dat's vy Herr Schneider talks so funny," Rosie said, "him and his buddy der Kaiser."

We all laughed and started talking with German accents.

"Hey," Rosie said, "if you promise to keep it a secret, I'll tell you what my brother Mike and his friends did last night."

After Jane and I crossed our hearts and hoped to die, Rosie beckoned us closer. "They threw a rock through the butcher shop window," she whispered, "and then they wrote *Kaiser Lover* and *Dirty Hun* on the sidewalk."

Jane looked worried. "If anybody finds out what they did, they'll be in so much trouble."

Rosie shrugged. "They ought to get a medal," she said.

"Everybody knows Herr Schneider wants the Kaiser to win the war."

I pictured Mr. Schneider — Herr Schneider — standing behind the meat case, wearing a bloodstained apron. He had the same squinty eyes as Elsie, but his nose looked like a big red potato stuck in the middle of his face. He could easily be a spy, a tattletale just like Elsie, only on a much bigger scale, tattling war secrets to the Kaiser. Ooooh, it gave me shivers.

"Follow me!" Rosie darted down Third Avenue, and Jane and I ran after her.

"Where are you going?" I shouted.

"To the butcher shop." Rosie laughed and ran on, sure we'd follow her.

Jane shot me a worried look, but I ran so fast I caught up with Rosie and then dashed past her. Behind us I heard Jane shout, "Wait for me!"

At the butcher shop, we saw a crowd of boys yelling insults. The Hun stood in the doorway, wearing his bloody butcher's apron and shaking his fist. "You boys," he yelled. "I know who you are. I tell your parents. They pay for busted window!"

A board covered the broken glass. On it, someone had painted *HUN* in huge, badly written letters.

Rosie ran into the crowd and began singing our favorite patriotic song, and Jane and I joined in.

> *Over there, over there,*
> *Send the word, send the word over there —*
> *That the Yanks are coming,*
> *The Yanks are coming,*
> *The drums rum-tumming everywhere.*
> *So prepare, say a prayer,*
> *Send the word, send the word to beware.*
> *We'll be over, we're coming over,*
> *And we won't come back till it's over*
> *Over there.*

We sang that song every morning in school right after we pledged allegiance to the flag. Filled with patriotic spirit, we emphasized *Yanks* so Herr Schneider couldn't fail to get the meaning. It was such a good performance that the boys stopped jeering and sang with us.

But we didn't linger. Linking arms, we marched past Schneider's Butcher Shop and turned the corner. None of us, not even Rosie, wanted our parents to hear about our behavior.

We hadn't gone a block before we saw Elsie coming

toward us eating a chocolate ice cream cone. She didn't see us until Rosie ran past her and knocked the ice cream out of her hand.

Jane and I ran after Rosie, and I bumped Elsie so hard she almost fell down. "Hun!" we shouted. "Kaiser lover!"

We formed a circle around her. "Something stinks." Rosie wrinkled her nose. "Fee fi fo fum, I smell the blood of a dirty Hun."

Around and around we went, trapping Elsie in a circle and chanting, "Fee fi fo fum, I smell the blood of a dirty Hun!"

"I'm telling Miss Harrison!" she screamed.

"You better not, you big fat crybaby," Rosie yelled. "We'll get you if you do!"

With that, the three of us broke apart and ran down the street and around the first corner. When Elsie was out of sight, we sat down on a curb. We were hot and tired and thirsty. I'd have paid ten dollars for an ice-cold glass of Coca-Cola.

"Do you think she'll tell?" Jane asked.

"So what if she does?" Rosie asked. "We'll just say she's lying. Everybody knows she lies about everything."

"But what if Miss Harrison believes Elsie?" Jane asked, her forehead scrunched into wrinkles of worry.

We sat there for a while, thinking about the trouble

we'd be in if Elsie convinced Miss Harrison we'd bullied her. She'd probably call our parents, and our parents —well, none of us dared to picture the punishments they might dish out for misbehaving in public.

Suddenly, Rosie jumped up. "Oh, my golly, I have to go home," she said. "Ma told me to mind Bridget after school, and I totally forgot."

Jane and I watched Rosie dash down the street, her red hair flashing in the afternoon sunlight. She lived six blocks away on the other side of town, but Jane lived near me, so we walked home together.

"Sometimes I feel sorry for Elsie," Jane said. "It must be awful not to have any friends."

"She brings it on herself, you know." Even as I spoke, I remembered the way Elsie had looked at me, holding hands with Rosie — me, her former best friend, her only friend. I reminded myself of what she'd done to Antoinette, but I couldn't erase the memory of Elsie's face, her mouth smeared with chocolate ice cream, the sugar cone lying on the sidewalk, a dribble of melting ice cream puddled around it.

"It's not her fault her father's a German," Jane said.

"Nobody liked her *before* the war," I said. "At least that's what Rosie says."

"I guess that's true. She's always been —" Jane

hesitated, trying to come up with the right word. "Different, I guess, as if she doesn't know how to fit in. She's on the outside, like that game we used to play when we were little — go in and out the window. Nobody wanted to be her partner. No matter what game we played, she was always the last to be chosen. It was kind of sad, but . . ."

By now we'd reached Jane's corner. Before she turned to go home, she said, "I guess Elsie will always be Elsie. Maybe we shouldn't pick on her so much."

"Maybe," I said, and she waved goodbye, leaving me to walk home alone.

Jane was just too nice sometimes. Rosie wasn't about to stop picking on Elsie. And neither was I, even though I felt a bit guilty about it.

I scuffled home through the piles of fallen leaves, thinking about the coming weekend and what Rosie and Jane and I might do. Sometimes we roller-skated down High Street, which was very steep and scary, but Rosie led the way and we followed. So far I had plenty of scabs on my knees from falls, but nothing worse.

If we didn't feel like roller-skating, we'd seesaw and swing in the park or play one, two, three O'Leario. Rosie and I either tied or one of us edged the other by one or two points. There were trees to climb and creeks to follow and woods to explore. If it rained, we'd go to the library and look for Tom Swift adventure books. Every once in a while, we found one we hadn't read. Rosie liked Zane Grey's western novels, and we acted them out in the park, riding make-believe horses and shooting make-believe guns.

Rosie always had ideas. She was never bored, and neither were we. She was the best friend I'd ever had.

SIX

AFTER SUPPER ONE NIGHT, Mother, Father, and I gathered in the living room as usual. Mother picked up the sweater she was knitting for me. The yarn was soft, and its color matched my eyes. Despite the lingering heat, I could hardly wait for her to finish it.

I settled down beside her with *Anne of Green Gables*. I was already halfway through it, and still thinking how much alike Rosie and Anne were. Maybe it was their red hair that made them so mischievous. I twirled a strand of my hair around my finger. Brown. Such a boring color. If only it were red. I couldn't imagine why Anne hated her hair when I would have traded my heart and soul for it.

Father sat nearby in his armchair reading the *Evening*

Sun. Suddenly he laid the paper down and looked at Mother. "It says here that the influenza epidemic is getting worse. Over *five hundred* cases were reported today in Philadelphia alone. The numbers are increasing in Baltimore, as well. As for New York and Boston, the hospitals don't have room for more patients, and undertakers are running out of coffins. In some places, they stack the bodies up in piles until they can bury them properly."

I stared in horror at Father. Dead bodies in piles? Were they outside where everyone could see them? No, they couldn't be. They must keep them in hospital basements or somewhere private. Morgues maybe. The very word made me shiver. How would I go to sleep tonight?

Mother didn't look up from her knitting. "Oh, Horace, you're frightening Annie. You know as well as I do how reporters exaggerate. The number is probably less than half what the newspapers say. As for bodies stacked in piles, that's ridiculous." She reached over and patted my hand.

Father shook his head. "It's very contagious, Ida, and there's no cure."

Mother frowned and laid down her knitting. "The flu comes and goes every year. Very few people die of it. In a month or so, it will be over, and so will the war, and everything will be back to normal."

"I'm not so sure." Father sighed and returned his attention to the newspaper. "This isn't the regular flu. It's much worse."

Mother hugged me. "Don't let your father worry you, Annie. If you catch the flu, you'll be well again in a week or less."

I hoped Mother was right, but no matter what she said, over five hundred cases in one day sounded worrisome to me. And if hospitals didn't have room for them, where would sick people go? And how long would the dead wait to be buried?

At recess the next day, we gathered in groups and talked about the Spanish influenza. All of a sudden, it was even bigger news than the war. And much closer to home. People were dying in Baltimore. Mount Pleasant was just outside the city.

"Our minister says it's God's punishment for the war in Europe," Eunice said.

"If that's true, only the Germans should catch it," Rosie said. "They started the war. They're the ones who ought to be punished."

Lucy shook her head. "My father says it's like the bubonic plague. It could wipe out almost the entire human race."

Rosie shook her head. "I don't believe that."

"My father knows more about it than you, Miss Smarty," Lucy said. "He's a *doctor*."

"Nobody has died in Mount Pleasant," Polly Anderson said.

"Then how come I saw a funeral procession on the way to school this morning?" Eunice asked. "Six black horses were pulling a hearse on Prospect Street, and at least six carriages followed it."

"I saw a black wreath on somebody's door on Maple Street," Lucy added. "That means somebody died in that house."

"My pop says you can feel perfectly fine in the morning," Rosie put in. "But then in the afternoon you start feeling bad, and by that night, you're *dead*."

"Can't we talk about something else?" Jane asked.

No one paid any attention to her. It seemed almost everyone had something to say about the influenza.

While we were talking, I noticed Elsie sitting a few feet away listening to us. The October sunlight glinted on her blond braids, turning flyaway wisps white.

Suddenly she turned her head and caught me looking at her. Our eyes locked. I couldn't look away. It was if she'd put a spell on me.

"What are *you* looking at?" Rosie asked Elsie.

"Nothing." Elsie stood up and walked away, and the spell broke.

Jane took my hand and peered into my eyes. "Are you all right, Annie?"

"I'm fine. Why?"

"I don't know. You have that look my mother talks about. You know, as if someone walked on your grave."

"That's creepy, Jane."

The bell rang and we hurried to form a line at the school door. While we filed into the classroom, my legs trembled, and I was glad to take my seat.

I didn't look at Elsie for the rest of the day, but I felt her eyes crawling up and down my back. Let her stare. I'd never be her friend again.

The next day at recess, Rosie taught us a new jump rope chant:

> *I had a little bird,*
> *And its name was Enza.*
> *I opened up the window,*
> *And in flew Enza.*

At first nobody understood the joke, so Rosie had to explain. "It's about catching the flu. In flew Enza — *influenza.*"

"Oh," Eunice said. "The little bird flies in your window, and you get the flu."

"That's right," Rosie said. "Go to the head of the class."

Lucy and Jane grabbed the jump rope and started turning, faster and faster. We ran in and skipped rope while the others chanted the Enza rhyme. When we missed, we caught flu and had to lie down on the ground and pretend to be dead.

Shivering with fear that I'd miss, I ran in, jumped without missing, and ran out of the rope's swing. "Hooray for me," I cried. "Enza didn't get me!"

Polly came after me and missed. She fell on the ground and cried, "Alas, I am dead and cannot take the math test tomorrow!"

Rosie laughed when it was her turn. "Enza can't catch me," she shouted as she jumped in, skipped rope, and darted out again. "I'm too fast for Enza," she boasted.

Elsie watched us from the sidelines. Looking directly at Rosie, she shouted, "I hope you catch the flu. You won't brag then."

"Dirty Hun," Rosie shouted back. "You're the one who should get the flu, not me. You're too fat to get away from Enza."

"I hope you die of the flu!" Elsie screamed. "It would serve you right!"

Forgetting jump rope, we all began yelling at Elsie. She retreated to the school's front steps before yelling back at us. We called her names. She called us names. All the girls joined in, shouting Elsie down. Louder and louder, insults bounced off the wall.

Miss Harrison opened the school door and saw what was happening. "Girls, girls!" she cried. "This is not the way Pearce students behave!"

"Rosie started it," Elsie shouted. "She said I was fat and she hoped I died of the flu!"

Miss Harrison frowned at Rosie. "Shame on you for saying such a hateful thing."

"Elsie's lying," Eunice shouted. "*She's* the one who started it. She said she hoped Rosie would die of the flu."

"*You're* the liar!" Elsie's round face turned red with anger. "I didn't say that!"

We all began shouting then. Elsie was a Hun. Her father loved the Kaiser, she loved the Kaiser, she was a stinking, dirty German, and she was spreading flu germs all over school.

Miss Harrison looked shocked and angry. "I will not tolerate this behavior. Line up and return to the classroom immediately."

As we got into line, Rosie muttered, "Recess is over early, and it's all Elsie's fault."

Once we were seated at our desks, Miss Harrison said, "I know you're worried about the flu, girls. Maybe we should talk about it. Does anyone have a question?"

Theresa Luciano raised her hand first. "My aunt says everybody who gets flu dies. Is that true?"

"Of course not, Theresa. Many people recover, but we hear more about the ones who die. Sometimes I think newspapers like to scare us."

"That's just what my mother says," I told Miss Harrison.

"What are the symptoms?" Eloise Murphy asked.

"From what I understand, it begins like any other flu — fever, fatigue, muscle and joint pain, headache, lack of appetite. Maybe a cough and a runny nose." Miss Harrison paused a moment. "It's just that the symptoms are more severe than normal, as is the flu itself."

Rosie raised her hand. "My pop says big cities are closing schools. Will our school close?"

"In many cities, they've closed theaters, department stores, and other places where large crowds gather — including schools."

"But *this* school." Rosie leaned forward eagerly. "Will *this* school close?"

"It's under discussion," Miss Harrison said. "The public schools closed yesterday, so I wouldn't be surprised if we follow suit."

Rosie sat back and grinned. "No more homework," she whispered to Jane in a voice loud enough for all of us to hear.

"Well," Elsie said, "I hope school stays open. Education is important, isn't it, Miss Harrison?"

Miss Harrison said, yes, of course it was. "But if our health is endangered, the school will close." She had to speak loudly to make herself heard over the murmur of dislike directed at Elsie.

After school, Rosie, Jane, Lucy, Eunice, and I headed to the corner grocer for candy. Turkish toffee was my current favorite, but the others were in favor of licorice — black for Rosie and red for Jane, Eunice, and Lucy.

Rosie chewed a big mouthful and opened her mouth wide. "Look, my teeth are black!"

"Mine are red," Lucy shouted. "Oh, I'm bleeding, help me, I'm bleeding to death!"

"Call for the doctor," I yelled. "Call for the nurse!"

Rosie, Eunice, and Jane joined in for the third line. "Call for the lady with the alligator purse!"

Lucy staggered about, gasping as if she were dying. Our laughter rang against the brick walls of the houses.

"Oh, no, it's the flu!" Rosie screamed. "Enza got Lucy!"

Just as Lucy fell down dead on the sidewalk, a door flew open and a woman came out on the front step. "Stop that noise this minute. Don't you girls have any respect? People are sick in this house. They need rest!"

For once, no one had anything smart to say, not even Rosie. Lucy leapt to her feet, and we all ran across the street and around a corner.

Ahead of us, a horse-drawn hearse waited in front of a house with a funeral wreath on its door. We stopped so fast we almost fell over each other. I tried to look away, but my eyes took in every detail — the hearse's ornate carvings, its shiny black paint, the sleek black horses, the black plumes on their heads, the driver in his black top hat, black over-coat, and white gloves.

Two men dressed in black came down the front steps carrying a coffin and slid it into the back of the hearse. The horses shuffled their feet and showed the whites of their eyes as if they knew death was in the box.

Rosie and Jane bowed their heads and made the sign of the cross. Lucy, Eunice, and I whispered a prayer.

The family followed the coffin down the steps. Mother, father, and two girls, all four dressed in black. Supported by her husband's arm, the woman sobbed into a handkerchief.

They climbed into a black carriage behind the hearse. Slowly, with great dignity, the horses walked past us. We watched the procession until it disappeared around a corner.

"Oh, mercy, that's the Jenkinses' house," Jane whispered. "Their son is my brother's age." She looked at us. "He wasn't with them, just his big sisters. Do you think Charlie died?" Her voice dropped, and she began to cry.

We gathered around Jane to comfort her. When she stopped crying, we walked slowly toward home. No one laughed, no one sang about Enza or the lady with the alligator purse. We passed two more funeral wreaths.

At one house, three women dressed in black knocked at a door. A woman with a sad face welcomed them inside. "Thank you for coming," the woman said as the door closed behind them.

"It's a viewing," Eunice whispered. "The dead person is right there in the parlor, so people can view him."

"Oh, no, that's awful. I could never go in a house and see a dead person in a coffin." Jane reached for my hand. Hers was cold, but I held it tightly. Enza had come to Mount Pleasant, bringing death with her.

"Have any of you seen a dead person?" Rosie asked.

"When my grandma died, I was only five," Lucy said,

"but my mother made me kiss her goodbye. She was cold and hard, like a statue." She shuddered. "I had nightmares for weeks afterward."

"I saw my Uncle Bert," Rosie said. "We had the wake at our house. Everybody talked and told stories and sang. It was a big party. They ate enough to feed the city of Baltimore, Ma said, and the men got so drunk they could scarcely walk. They forgot about poor Uncle Bert all alone in the spare room. I went in and looked at him, but I was too scared to get closer than the doorway."

Jane, Eunice, and I had never been to a viewing, much less seen a dead person, so we had no stories to add.

We walked another block before coming to the corner where we split up to walk our separate ways home.

"Wait a minute," Rosie said. "I have an idea."

We turned to her, all four of us, and waited. Rosie hesitated a moment, almost as if she thought we might not like what she was about to say.

"I was just thinking about my uncle's wake and all the food — especially the cakes and pies and cookies and candy. Yes, chocolate candy, the kind that comes in fancy boxes, and some are delicious and others you spit out when nobody's looking."

We nodded. Everybody knew that kind of candy. It

appeared at Christmas usually. Just thinking about it made my mouth water.

"Well." Rosie paused again. "What if we went to viewings and pretended we knew the dead person? Just think about all the sweets we'd get."

"Oh, Rosie, no," Jane said. "We can't go to a viewing just to get sweets."

"We'd be taking advantage of people." That's what I said, but I really meant I didn't want to see dead people or be in the same house where someone died of the flu — what if their germs were still in the furniture and the drapes and the carpet and maybe even the refreshments?

"We'd be pretending to know the dead person," Jane added. "And that's the same as lying."

"We won't be doing anything wrong," Rosie said. "We'll tell people how sorry we are, we'll talk about how nice the dead person was, we'll make the mourners feel better. That's not taking advantage, that's not lying."

"We'll be polite and well behaved." To demonstrate, Lucy lowered her head piously.

Eunice nodded. "And then we'll have some refreshments and leave."

"And just think of the money we'll save if we get free candy instead of buying it at the corner grocery," Rosie said.

Eunice looked at Jane. "Nobody said you have to come with us. Or you either, Annie. You can spend your allowance on candy if you want to."

She and Lucy stood on either side of Rosie, their arms linked with hers. I gave Jane a worried look. "We didn't say we weren't coming, we just —"

"You're just scared to see a dead person," Rosie said.

Jane and I drew closer together. In the look that passed between us, we read each other's minds. If we backed out of Rosie's plan, Lucy and Eunice would take our places as Rosie's best friends.

"Think of the cakes," Eunice said, "and the cookies."

"And the chocolate candy with caramel or nougat in the middle." Rosie smacked her lips.

Think of the coffin, I wanted to add, *standing in a dark corner, its top open so everyone can see the dead body. Think of the flu germs in the cake.*

"So everyone is in?" Rosie asked.

Jane and I nodded slowly. We were in, mainly because neither of us wanted to be out.

"Well," Rosie said, "it's almost suppertime. Read the obituaries tonight. Tomorrow we'll pick which houses to visit."

Rosie ran down Prospect Street toward home. The

rest of us turned the corner and headed up Hill Street. Eunice and Lucy chattered about the sweets we'd have, but Jane and I said little. I sensed she was just as worried as I was.

After Eunice and Lucy went their way, Jane squeezed my hand. "Do you think we should meet them tomorrow?"

"If we don't, Rosie won't be friends with us."

Jane sighed. "We have to stick together, don't we?"

"We won't look at the dead person, we won't even get near the coffin," I said. "We'll just eat a cookie and leave."

"Maybe she'll change her mind," Jane said. "Maybe we won't have to do it after all."

We both knew there was no chance of that. Once Rosie made up her mind, it stayed made up. And besides, she loved sweets. How could she resist the opportunity to get them for free?

I waved goodbye to Jane and trudged down Portman Street alone. It was almost dark. A cold wind stirred the fallen leaves. They seemed to rise up and follow me, tip tapping like ghostly shoes on the sidewalk, whispering among themselves.

I walked faster, suddenly afraid of the leaves scurrying at my heels. I wanted to look over my shoulder, but I was scared of what I might see following close behind me. It was as if the ghosts of Enza's victims had risen from their graves to carry me away with them, far from my home, my parents, my friends, my life.

Tomorrow I'd say no to Rosie. I wouldn't go near the dead, not for all the free sweets in the world.

SEVEN

THE NEXT DAY I came downstairs dressed for school only to be told Pearce Academy was closed until the flu ran its course.

"The department stores on Main Street are closed too," Mother said, "and so are the churches and movie theaters. No Liberty Bond parade this weekend either."

I sat down and stared at her. "No school?" I'd worked past bedtime on the report due today. Now it seemed I might as well have read *Riders of the Purple Sage* instead.

"Two hundred and eighty-nine people died in Philadelphia yesterday." Mother wrung the dishcloth in her hands, letting the water drip on the floor. "That's almost three hundred people in one day, Annie."

I stirred sugar into my oatmeal. When I swallowed the first spoonful, my throat felt scratchy. I was tired, listless. Appetite gone, I pushed my bowl away.

"What's wrong, Annie?" Mother asked. "Don't you want your oatmeal?"

I shook my head. "I don't feel well. I think I'm getting sick."

Mother felt my forehead, her way of checking my temperature. "You're as cool as a cucumber," she said with a smile. "You're worried about the flu, aren't you?"

"It comes on very quickly, you know."

"Yes," Mother said. "But we mustn't dwell on it. It's bad for you."

"Maybe we should wear flu masks. Lots of people have them now."

Mother laughed. "Don't be silly. Your father says those things are worthless. That flimsy little piece of gauze won't stop germs."

Still feeling a little uncertain about my health, I returned to my room and changed into play clothes. Perhaps I'd take it easy today. Stay home. Rest. I'd tell Rosie I couldn't go to any viewings because I was sick.

I'd no sooner curled up with *Purple Sage* than I heard the doorbell chime. Mother called upstairs to say Jane was there. I laid the book down as Jane came running up the steps.

"We're supposed to meet Rosie and the others at noon in front of 28 Prospect Street," she told me.

"How do you know that?"

"Rosie telephoned. She tried to call you too, but Mrs. Cooper was hogging your party line with gossip about the flu."

Now was the time to tell Jane I wasn't going, but if I stayed home and everyone else went, they'd think I was scared. They might tease me. They might even stop being friends with me. Then what would I do?

So I followed Jane downstairs. Mother stopped us at the door to ask where we were going.

"Oh," I said, trying to sound casual, "we're meeting Rosie, Lucy, and Eunice at the park."

It was the first time I'd ever lied to Mother, and I was shocked to discover how easy it was.

"Have fun," Mother called after us. "It's a lovely day. Enjoy the sunshine and fresh air."

As soon as the front gate closed behind us, Jane asked, "Are you scared?"

"Oh, perhaps little bit." Another lie — I was terrified. "Are you?"

"Yes," Jane said. "I'm not going near the coffin. I'll sit

on the other side of the room. I doubt I'll be able to eat anything. It's just not right."

"We could always say we're not going."

"We have to go, Annie. We said we would."

Holding hands, we walked toward Prospect Street. "Do
you think we're dressed all right?" Jane asked.

We were both wearing play clothes. My dress was dark
blue with a dropped waist and a sailor collar, and Jane's was
black and white plaid with a pleated skirt. We wore long
black stockings and high-top button shoes, and our hair was
combed and held back with ribbons tied in big bows.

"I hope so," I said. "We can't very well go out to play in
our Sunday best."

No matter how slowly we walked, we came to Prospect
Street. Rosie, Lucy, and Eunice were waiting in front of a
house with a big black wreath on the door. We paused and
took a deep breath. While we hesitated, several mourners
passed us and climbed the front steps. They knocked softly.
As the door opened, the murmur of voices drifted out of the
house.

"Look sad," Rosie told Jane and me. "Tell Mrs. O'Neil
how sorry you are to learn of her daughter's passing —"

"Don't say death or dying," Eunice butted in. "It's
rude."

Rosie led us up the steps. "I hope they have something

good, chocolates maybe," she whispered, and then knocked softly.

The door opened, and a woman with a kind but sorrowful face welcomed us inside.

"We are so sad about Agnes," Rosie said. "We'll miss hearing her sing in the church choir."

"Thank you, dear." Mrs. O'Neil pressed Rosie's hand between hers.

The parlor was crowded with people, all strangers to us, speaking in low voices. Followed by Lucy and Eunice, Rosie approached the coffin, which rested on a platform in a little alcove that might have been designed exactly for that purpose. She pinched my arm and gave Jane and me a warning look.

I glanced at Jane, and she at me. With a small shrug, or perhaps it was a shiver, Jane walked slowly to the coffin with me close behind. Rosie stood beside it, looking like a statue in the cemetery, her head slightly lowered and a pious expression on her face. All she needed was a pair of wings sprouting from her shoulder blades.

Although I lingered behind Jane and did not look too closely, I glimpsed a pale but beautiful face, eyes closed, hair arranged in a swirl of dark curls across a satin pillow. Agnes didn't look exactly alive, but she didn't look exactly dead either. In truth, she was not as scary as I'd imagined she'd be. I felt overwhelmingly sad to see her lie so still. My eyes brimmed with tears, and I turned away.

"There, there." A woman gave me a little hug. "Don't be sad, dear. Agnes is at peace with the Lord."

At first I thought she said Agnes was at the beach with the Lord, and I stared at her in amazement. Then I understood and lowered my eyes.

"Would you like some cake?" the woman asked.

I followed her to a table covered with an embroidered cloth and laden with food — slices of yellow cake with rich chocolate icing, dozens of sugar cookies, gingersnaps, and dainty madeleines, a big crystal bowl of red punch.

"Help yourself, sweetheart."

I wasn't hungry, but to be polite, I took a small slice of cake and retreated to a corner as far away from the coffin as possible.

Jane joined me. She'd taken a piece of cake and a cookie, but like me she toyed with the food.

Across the room, Rosie was talking to Mr. and Mrs. O'Neil about Agnes and her lovely voice that no one would ever hear again and wasn't that the saddest thing.

"How does she know so much about Agnes?" I whispered to Jane.

"She read the obituary," Jane whispered back.

The next time I looked her way, Rosie was talking

about Agnes's charity, how she gave to the poor and helped with fundraising for wounded veterans coming home from Europe, and volunteered in a school for immigrant children.

"I plan to use Agnes as a model," Rosie told the weeping O'Neils. "I will do my best to emulate her and take up charity work myself."

Lucy joined us, her face flushed with suppressed laughter. "I think we should leave before I lose my self control and burst into a fit of giggles."

Eunice tugged at Rosie's arm and whispered something to her. "Oh yes, oh thank you for reminding me, Eunice."

Turning back to the O'Neils, she told them once again of her admiration for Agnes and apologized for needing to leave. "I have a dental appointment," she told them.

The O'Neils hugged Rosie and thanked her for coming and claimed her remarks had done them a world of good. The crowd of mourners looked our way and smiled tenderly. I could almost hear them thinking what sweet, well-behaved girls we were.

Once we were outside, I took a deep breath. "How could you tell them all those things, Rosie? You never saw Agnes O'Neil until today, and her lying in her coffin, at that."

Rosie looked surprised. "You heard what the O'Neils said. I made them feel better. How can you find fault with that?"

"And we made ourselves feel better," Eunice added, "by stuffing ourselves with sweets."

Eunice was already plump, but I didn't tell her what I thought — if she kept eating sweets at viewings, she'd need a new wardrobe before Christmas.

After that, we attended at least two viewings a day. With schools and stores and movie theaters closed, what else were we to do?

The dead were strangers, mostly young because that was who Enza preferred — young people in their teens and twenties, some older and some younger, a few much older and a few much younger. The saddest was a toddler barely three years old. She looked like a baby doll, and I was tempted to pick her up and rock her.

Yes, I'd gotten quite used to the dead, so silent, so still, nothing frightening about them after all.

We took care to memorize obituaries so we'd say the right things. How talented artistically or musically, how charitable, how courteous and thoughtful. Never angry. Never mean. No wonder the Lord took them to his bosom, saving them perhaps from future misery.

At night I'd lie in bed and wonder what people would say of me if I died of the flu. I was pretty certain I'd be portrayed as saintly as the other dearly departed. Unless they asked Elsie. She'd make up horrible stories about me. She'd say I was a bad friend. She'd say I was mean to her. She'd lie and say I cheated on tests and copied my homework and stole candy from the corner grocery.

Oh, yes, if I died, Elsie would make up plenty of bad things to say about me.

EIGHT

ONE DAY in that awful autumn of death and funerals and fear, we were walking home from a particularly dreadful viewing — identical twin girls, six years old, laid out in the same coffin, their arms around each other as if they were sleeping. We hadn't stayed long enough to eat more than one cookie.

Jane was still crying when Rosie stopped so suddenly I bumped into her. "Look who I see."

She pointed at the park across the street. Elsie was sitting in a swing all by herself, spinning idly, too lazy to push off and soar treetop high.

Lucy giggled. "She's wearing a flu mask."

"Too bad it doesn't hide her whole ugly face," Eunice said.

We started to walk on, but Rosie remained where she was and stared hard at Elsie. "She got me in trouble the last day of school. Let's get even."

Before we could agree or disagree, Rosie charged across the street, whooping like an Indian on the warpath. We followed her, whooping as loudly as we could.

Elsie looked up and saw us coming. She jumped out of the swing and began to run across the park. She was big, but she was clumsy and she couldn't run fast enough to escape us. Rosie caught her, yanked off her flu mask, and put it on her own face.

"Enza's coming for you!" she said to Elsie. "She's going to fly in your window tonight. By tomorrow morning, you'll be dead!"

"And no one will be sorry. No one will miss you," Lucy added, "because nobody likes you."

"You're mean and you're a liar and you're a big fat Hun!" Eunice yelled.

At that, Rosie told us to join hands in a circle, trapping Elsie inside. Round and round we went, faster and faster, chanting,

I had a little bird,
And its name was Enza.

I opened up the window,
And in flew Enza.

The faster we went, the faster we sang, laying particular emphasis on "in flew Enza."

Elsie ran against us, trying to break her way out of the circle, but we held firm. She couldn't escape. "Let me out," she cried. "I want to go home!"

"In flew Enza, in flew Enza," we shouted. "Had a little bird, name was Enza, opened window, IN FLEW ENZA!"

"I'll tell my mother on you!"

"I'll tell my mother on you, I'll tell my mother on you," Rosie echoed in a perfect imitation of Elsie's voice.

We were hysterical, we couldn't stop. Even when Elsie sank to the ground, crying, we couldn't stop. Round and round and round her, we ran screaming "IN FLEW ENZA," until our throats were sore and we were almost too dizzy to stand up.

Finally we broke apart and reeled across the grass, falling into piles of autumn leaves, gasping for breath.

For a moment, Elsie crouched on the ground. She seemed smaller somehow, a rabbit caught by a pack of dogs. Suddenly she looked up and caught me staring at her. Our eyes locked just as they had before. This time, I turned away quickly, ashamed of myself, of all of us.

Elsie scrambled awkwardly to her feet and ran, her arms flapping, knock-kneed, as clumsy as a baby elephant, only much more pathetic.

Following Rosie's lead, we chased Elsie again, shouting and jeering, myself included, despite my guilty feelings.

"You can't run from Enza," Rosie yelled.

We stopped on the edge of the park and watched Elsie cross Prospect Street. She ran more slowly now, her head down. One braid had come loose, and the bow on her dress was untied. She looked so pitiful I turned my head away, afraid she'd catch me staring again. I couldn't bear the sadness in her eyes.

"Run, baby, run!" Rosie shouted. "Run home to Mama!" Turning to us with a laugh, she said, "I guess we taught her a lesson!"

She was still wearing Elsie's mask, and it made her look scary.

Lucy snatched the mask from Rosie and put it on. Eunice grabbed it from Lucy. Rosie tried to get it back.

Jane and I watched the three girls play keep away with the mask, but we didn't join in. For both of us, the fun had gone out of the day.

At last Rosie tossed the mask aside as if it were a dead rat. "Let's go," she said.

Without linking arms, we walked slowly across the park, almost deserted in the late afternoon light. Rosie started singing the Enza song, but only Eunice joined in.

I found myself thinking of Elsie crouched on the grass, as helpless as a baby bird. To keep from feeling sorry for her, I reminded myself of what she'd done to my doll and the times she'd tried to get me in trouble with Miss Harrison.

Yes, I thought, *Elsie deserved what we'd done to her.*

But why did the sight of her flu mask lying in the leaves make me feel sad?

Less than a week later, we were walking down Third Avenue. November had arrived and brought the promise of winter with it. A cold wind sneaked up behind us and crept through the gap between our collars and our necks. It pinched our noses and the tips of our fingers. It seeped up from the pavement, right through the soles of our shoes, and chilled our toes.

We planned to go to a viewing on the other side of the park, a long walk on such a windy day.

"I hate cold weather," Eunice grumbled.

"But not if it snows," Rosie said. "Since school's closed, we can sled ride all day long." She grinned. "Pop says the *Farmer's Almanac* is calling for tons of snow and a long winter."

"And don't forget the woolly bear caterpillars," Jane said. "Every one I've seen has a really narrow brown stripe."

"Ugh." Eunice shivered. "I hope the almanac is wrong, wrong, wrong."

While we stood on the corner, a funeral procession came toward us. We waited on the curb and watched a pair of black horses walk slowly past, pulling the hearse. Their glossy necks arched, the black plumes on their heads waved in the breeze. Through the glass windows, I saw the coffin heaped with flowers. Behind it came a long procession of mourners, walking slowly, solemnly. They said nothing, but stared straight ahead. It scared me to watch them coming toward us, each step measured, their faces grim.

"Somebody important must have died," Eunice said.

"It's probably the mayor," Lucy said. "Father is his doctor. *Was* his doctor, I mean. He told us he'd died."

As soon as the last mourner passed by, Rosie said, "I guess he won't be boring the whole town with a long speech this Fourth of July."

"Don't be disrespectful," Lucy said.

Rosie shrugged. "I don't know about the rest of you, but I'm cold and hungry, and I don't feel like walking all the way to the other side of the park. Let's go to that house and get something to eat."

She pointed at a wreath on a door in the middle of the block. It was a small, shabby house in a row of small and shabby houses, and the wreath was so small we could have easily missed seeing it.

"It's not on our list," Eunice said.

"We don't know who lives there or who died," Jane added. "We might say the wrong thing."

"We've been doing this for three weeks now," Rosie said. "We'll make it up as we go along."

Jane and I exchanged looks, but before we had a chance to protest, Rosie walked boldly up the steps and knocked on the door.

A stern-looking woman invited us inside. "Thank you for coming. You must be my daughter's classmates."

"We're so sorry," Rosie said, not pausing for a second. It was if she'd memorized a script suitable for all occasions. "We'll miss her so much. She was so sweet. Everyone adored her."

I caught Eunice eying the refreshments and hoped the woman wouldn't notice.

"Come and say goodbye to her," the woman said.

All five of us arrived at the coffin at the same moment. No longer afraid to look at the dead, we leaned over the side to stare at the body. We all gasped, even Rosie, and backed away, almost tripping over our own feet.

Jane grabbed my hand and began to cry. I held her hand tightly, sure I was about to faint. To swoon. To collapse. My legs shook, and my arms trembled.

"You girls look frightened," the woman said. "Have you never seen a dead person?"

"It's such a shock," Rosie whispered, sounding sincere for once. Her face was so pale every freckle stood out. "We saw her just a few days ago."

Yes, I thought, *we saw her.* We chased her and made her our prisoner. We scared her with the Enza song, and Rosie told her she'd die that very night. She took Elsie's mask and wore it herself.

And now, less than a week later, Elsie lay in her coffin, never to open her eyes or speak again.

"Kneel down by her," Mrs. Schneider said. "Say a prayer for Elsie."

I wanted to run from the house and not stop until I got home, but like my friends, I knelt by the coffin.

My face was level with Elsie's porcelain hands, clasped as if in prayer. I stared at her fingers, white with a tinge of blue like snow. I knew I'd see them in my dreams for years to come.

I glanced at her face. It seemed as if her eyes were open a tiny slit. She was looking at me. No, of course she wasn't. It was a trick of the light.

Quickly I returned my gaze to her hands. It was safer to look at them than at her face. I stared at her pale fingers as if they held the secret of life and death. "Rest in peace, Elsie," I whispered. "Forgive me for being mean to you."

Slowly the five of us stood up and prepared to leave, but Mrs. Schneider stopped us with a question. "Did any of you see Elsie at the park last Wednesday? She came home in tears and told me a gang of girls called her names and chased her. They even stole her flu mask. I'd like to know who those girls are."

We shook our heads, we didn't know them, we hadn't seen them, Elsie was by herself, she was wearing her mask when we saw her.

Mr. Schneider stepped out of a corner and joined us. "I blame them girls for Elsie's death." He stared at us, his face as pale and stony as Elsie's. "If you hear anything, tell me. Their parents should know vat sort of daughters they haf."

I thought Jane was about to collapse right there and then. Her face was ashen, and her eyes brimmed with tears.

She opened her mouth as if to speak, and I seized her arm, afraid of what she might say.

"Jane isn't well," I whispered to Mrs. Schneider. "We should leave before she has one of her fainting spells."

Mrs. Schneider said, "She does look poorly. You can't take chances these days."

Mr. Schneider followed us to the door. "You tell me. I vant to know the names of them girls."

"Yes, sir," Rosie whispered. "Yes, we will."

He nodded, and we ran down the front steps as if Elsie herself pursued us.

When we were around the corner and out of sight of Elsie's house, we stopped to catch our breath. We hadn't eaten a thing at the viewing, but Rosie leaned over and threw up in the gutter, heaving and heaving until nothing but green bile came up.

Wiping her mouth with the back of her hand, she moaned and clutched her empty belly. "Oh, my God, it's my fault, it's all my fault."

Rosie began crying, something I'd never expected to see her do. We gathered around her, patting her back, stroking her hair, murmuring, but she ignored our attempts to comfort her. "Why did I tell her she'd die? Why did I take her flu mask?"

Eunice grabbed Rosie's hand and peered into her eyes.

"What's wrong with you? It's not your fault. It's not any-body's fault." She paused to take a breath. "She was mean, and she lied and tattled on us, and none of us liked her."

Rosie stared at Eunice. "Don't you feel bad about what we did? Don't you care she's dead?"

"Well, yes, of course, I care." Eunice backtracked, shifting her position to side with Rosie. "My goodness. I'm just saying it's not your fault or my fault. None of us is to blame. It was a game, that's all. We didn't know she'd die. We didn't make her die."

Rosie looked at Jane and me. "What do you think? Did I kill Elsie?"

"No," I said. "No." I was scared now.

Tears ran down Rosie's face, mixing with snot from her nose. "I'm going to hell when I die," she wailed.

Jane grabbed Rosie's arm. "You didn't mean to hurt El-sie, so it's not a mortal sin. Not the kind you go to hell for."

Lucy spoke up. "I don't believe in hell. Or the devil."

"Everyone believes in hell," Eunice said, "and the devil."

Lucy shook her head. "I'm Unitarian, and we don't be-lieve people are burned in hell. My father says a just God wouldn't do something that cruel."

"Our minister says Unitarians aren't even Christian," Eunice said.

Just as we were building up to a religious quarrel, a door opened and a man told us to please lower our voices. His wife had flu, and we were disturbing her rest.

After he closed the door, Rosie knuckled her tears away and sniffed. Jane took her hand and squeezed it gently. "Do you feel better now, Rosie?"

"I guess so," she said in a low voice, "but I still wish I hadn't taken her mask and said she'd die."

Eunice looked at all of us. "Let's promise never to tell anyone what happened in the park. If nobody tells, nobody will know, and we won't get in trouble."

Rosie spit in her palm, and we all did the same. Rubbing our hands together, we mixed our spit and swore we'd never tell.

We turned toward home. No one had anything to say. Rosie concentrated on kicking a stone down the sidewalk ahead of her. Jane huddled in her coat as if the autumn wind was as cold as winter. Eunice hummed "I Dream of Jeannie," an old Stephen Foster song we sang in school. Lucy kicked leaves aside hoping to find a penny or a nickel. And me — I tried to banish the image of Elsie in her coffin to a dark corner of my mind where I wouldn't have to see it.

First Rosie left us, then Eunice and Lucy. Jane and I walked on, still silent.

Finally Jane asked, "Do you think it's our fault, Annie?"

I shook my head. "Father would say it's a coincidence."

Jane nodded. "That must be it. Like we told Rosie, it's not anybody's fault Elsie died."

But she didn't sound any more certain than I was. What if it was our fault, what if we were all going to hell for what we did?

We lingered on Jane's corner as if we were afraid to part and go our separate ways. The days were short now, and darkness seemed to creep out of the earth itself. The wind had picked up, and I was cold in the thin jacket I'd put on when I left home.

"Well," Jane said, "the streetlights are on, and my parents will be worried about me. I'd better go home."

I watched her walk away, her head down, her footsteps muffled by the fallen leaves. She looked sad and lonely and very small under the row of tall trees bending over the road.

After she disappeared from sight, I pictured a day when I'd be older and my life would be different, and Jane and I wouldn't be best friends anymore. We might live far apart. I might never know her future, or she mine.

As I went on alone, I promised myself I wouldn't think about Elsie Schneider lying in her coffin. Her eyes weren't open, not even a slit. She hadn't looked at me. She hadn't, hadn't, *had not* looked at me. She couldn't have. She was dead. Dead. And she was never coming back.

But why did I glance over my shoulder? Why did I imagine I heard footsteps behind me? Why did I run the rest of the way home?

NINE

THAT NIGHT I had little appetite for supper. Mother looked at me with concern. "What's wrong, Annie? Don't you feel well?"

Truthfully, I did not feel well. My throat definitely felt scratchy. I had a tiny dry cough. And I felt hot. Flu symptoms, I was certain of it. I'd caught it from Elsie, my punishment for scaring her and making her cry.

Father's head came up, and he too looked at me. "Check her temperature, Ida," he said.

This time, Mother did not feel my forehead. She went straight to the bathroom and came back with a thermometer. "Under your tongue," she said as she slid it between my teeth. "And keep your mouth closed."

When she removed the thermometer, she squinted at the little silver line, turning the thermometer this way and that, taking so long to make out the degrees that Father snatched it out of her hand.

"Ninety-eight point six," he said. "Just right."

I didn't have the flu. Not yet.

After dinner, I picked up my old copy of *Little Women* and turned to the description of Beth's death. Picturing the possibility of my own death, I began to cry, at first quietly, then louder.

Father looked up from the evening paper in alarm. "What on earth is wrong, Annie? It's just a book. Nothing to cry over."

Mother sat on the sofa beside me and stroked my hair. "Something has upset you," she murmured. "Is it the death of the Schneider girl?"

"How did you know?"

"Her obituary is in the *Evening Sun*."

I cuddled closer to Mother, seeking warmth and comfort. "How long are people contagious before they actually get the flu?"

Mother looked at me. "Were you around Elsie before she got sick?"

"We were in the park last week, I can't remember

exactly when, and we were playing. She didn't seem sick then."

Father looked at me over the paper. "I believe the incubation period is about three days, so if you saw her a week ago, you'd already have it."

"What if you touch something the person has, can you catch it that way?

"For example?" Father asked.

"Elsie was wearing a flu mask, and she let Rosie try it on. Lucy and Eunice tried it on, too."

"Did you and Jane try it on?" Father asked. The concern in his voice scared me.

"No. We were afraid of it. We didn't even touch it."

Father and Mother exchanged worried looks. "I'm glad you didn't put it on," Mother said.

"Do you think Rosie and Lucy and Eunice will catch the flu?"

"I hope not," Mother murmured, hugging me close again.

"Perhaps you shouldn't play with them for a few days," Father said.

"Horace, for heaven's sake," Mother said. "Don't frighten Annie with talk like that. You just said the incubation period was three days."

"*Usually* it's three days," Father said glumly, "but with this flu, who can be sure of anything?"

"Should I call the girls' mothers and advise them to keep an eye on their daughters?"

"Oh, I'm sure they'll be all right." Father backtracked hastily, probably so as not to worry me. "They were outside in the fresh air."

The phone rang and Mother hurried into the hall to answer it. I heard her murmuring but not clearly enough to understand what she was saying. Suppose it was Rosie's mother calling to say Rosie had died of the flu?

When Mother hung up, I was prickling all over, terrified of what she might say.

"That was Miss Harrison," Mother said, taking a seat beside me. "Elsie's funeral will be at the First Lutheran Church tomorrow. She hopes all the girls in her class will attend and sit together. Do you think you can muster the courage to go?"

"Of course she can," Father said behind his newspaper. "It's the proper thing to do."

"But Annie has never seen a dead person," Mother said. "And she's so sensitive."

Ashamed to look at my parents, I slid deeper into the sofa. I'd probably seen more dead people than both of them. Without making much of an effort, I began to cry again.

"Oh, Father, don't make me go," I begged. "I don't want to see Elsie. I can't bear it."

Through half-closed eyes, I saw them look at each other, obviously concerned. Mother shook her head, and Father shrugged.

"Of course you don't have to go," Mother said softly. "Unlike some parents, I've never believed children should be forced to attend funerals. Especially ones with delicate natures like you, Annie."

Feeling guilty, I went up to bed, but I lay awake a long time, thinking about Elsie's death and fearing my own. The wind blew around the house, and the windowpanes rattled as if someone were trying to get into my bedroom.

When I finally fell asleep, I dreamed that Elsie was sitting on my bed, watching me. When she leaned over me, her hair brushed my cheek and I felt the touch of her cold hand on my hand. She clasped Antoinette tightly.

"You think you're rid of me," she whispered, "but you're wrong. I'm still here, Annie." With that, she yanked off Antoinette's wig. Hundreds of worms slithered out of the hole in the doll's head.

I woke up screaming so loudly that Mother rushed into my room with Father behind her.

"What is it, Annie?" Mother cried, gathering me into her arms.

"Elsie," I cried. "Elsie was sitting on my bed, Mother, right where you're sitting now. She wasn't dead, she—" I couldn't go on.

Father patted my shoulder. "There, there, Annie. It was a dream, that's all. Try not to think about that poor girl."

Father went back to bed, but Mother sat with me awhile. "Would you like me to sing to you like I did when you were little?"

"Yes, please. Sing the lullaby about the western sea."

While I clung to her hand, she sang "Sweet and low, sweet and low, wind of the western sea."

Gradually I relaxed. With Mother beside me, I was safe. No harm could come to me. Elsie was gone. She wouldn't return. Couldn't return.

The next morning, church bells woke me up. Not funeral knells but wild ringing as if maniacs were swinging on the ropes. Frightened by the clanging of so many bells, I ran downstairs. Mother and Father grabbed my hands and laughed out loud.

"Don't look so worried, Annie!" Father said. "They signed the Armistice! The war is over!"

Mother looked at the kitchen clock. "Officially the celebration begins this morning on the eleventh hour, of the eleventh day, of the eleventh month," she said, "but the treaty was signed at five a.m. in France, and nobody's waiting until it's eleven a.m. here."

She opened the back door, and in came the cold November air, bringing with it the din of the bells. People cheered and fireworks exploded. Mother grabbed pots and lids and handed some to Father and me.

"Come on," she cried. "Let's add our part to the celebration."

We ran out into the street and joined our neighbors. Mr. Elliot from across the street was blowing a trumpet. His son, who played in the high school band, was pounding a drum and our next-door neighbor Mr. Higgins actually had a tuba. They were trying to play "Over There," and it sounded so horrible it was wonderful.

After the cold chased everyone back into their houses, Mother made hot chocolate, and we raised our mugs and drank a toast to Mother's brother, Paul, who'd be coming home soon. In celebration, Mother made pancakes and bacon and scrambled eggs. She even let us have slices of cake left over from dinner last night. By the time I finished eating, I thought my stomach would burst wide open.

It wasn't until I walked over to Jane's house that I realized I hadn't thought about Elsie once. Jane saw me coming and ran to meet me. "Let's go to Prospect Street and watch the parade," she cried.

Forgetting Elsie again, I ran with Jane toward the sounds of a real marching band playing the National Anthem. Mobs of happy people followed the band, singing and yelling and waving flags. Rosie caught up with us. She had her brother's police whistle and we took turns blowing it. Lucy and Eunice found us in the crowd, and we let ourselves be carried along, giddy with excitement.

The band turned a corner. They were playing "Alexander's Ragtime Band," and people were dancing in the street.

We passed the First Lutheran Church just as the pallbearers brought a coffin down the steps — a coffin too small for an adult. Mr. and Mrs. Schneider followed it, walking slowly, their heads down, their faces pale against their black clothing. Miss Harrison came close behind them, leading a group of our classmates. When she saw us in the crowd of revelers, she frowned.

The parade came to a halt, of course. The band stopped playing and bowed their heads. Men removed their hats and put their hands on their hearts. Women stood silently, their faces full of grief for their own losses.

Paralyzed with shock at the sight of Elsie's coffin, all four of us stood there in plain view. Mr. and Mrs. Schneider both saw us. For a moment I was afraid they were going to cross the street and confront us, but they shook their heads and climbed into the carriage behind the hearse.

Even after the funeral procession had vanished, the crowd spoke in low voices. The band marched away silently and didn't play until they were out of sight.

"Let's get out of here," Rosie said, but we weren't fast enough to escape Miss Harrison.

"I'm shocked to see you celebrating instead of attending Elsie's funeral." She looked at us in a way that made us all feel like monsters without consciences. "I truly thought better of you."

Her eyes moved from one of us to another. "I talked to your parents last night. I told them the time and the date. Everyone, except Annie's mother, said you'd be at the church with your classmates. Yet here you are, rowdy and rude, behaving like hoydens as if I'd never taught you proper etiquette. You have deeply disappointed me."

With that, she turned away, head up, back stiff, and joined the well-behaved girls waiting for her.

"Teacher's pets," Eunice muttered.

Nobody else had anything to say. We'd lost our enthusiasm for the parade. What was there to do but go home?

TEN

DURING THE MONTHS after Elsie's death, funeral knells still rang, but not five or six times a day as they had earlier. We didn't see as many hearses in the streets or funeral wreaths on doors. In December, school reopened and the four of us worked hard to win back Miss Harrison's approval. Besides Elsie, two girls at Pearce died of the flu, but they weren't in our class, and we didn't know them.

Uncle Paul came home for Christmas, but he shared no war stories with us. He was pale and thin and walked with a limp. He looked older, too. And he seemed uncertain about things. Even though he'd survived the war, Mother continued to worry about him.

A few days after Christmas, Uncle Paul caught a train to Ohio to live with my grandparents.

We stood on the platform waving until the train was out of sight. As we returned to the car, Mother took Father's arm. "He's not himself," she murmured.

"Perhaps with the passage of time," Father began, but dropped his voice so low I couldn't hear what he said next.

I dawdled behind them, knowing they didn't want me to overhear their worries. I'd seen the change for myself.

In January, the snow began. We went sledding every day after school and all day on weekends. High Street was our favorite. The hill was so steep you felt as if you were flying, but you had to be careful not to crash into the stone wall at the bottom.

A boy named Henry had been killed there last year. He fractured his skull and died instantly. Some kids claimed Henry's ghost haunted the place where he'd died. They said his ghost tried to make kids crash into the wall, but they just wanted to scare us.

A group of older kids kept a bonfire going at the top, and parents often provided marshmallows and hot chocolate. Best of all, our parents allowed us to stay out after dark as long as we were home by eight. We felt grown-up and daring and ready for adventures.

One night Rosie asked, "Are you getting tired of High Street?"

"Do you know a better place?" Lucy asked.

"Follow me!" Rosie grabbed her sled, did a perfect belly flop, and sped down the hill.

We flew behind her, our sled runners bouncing over the ruts made by other sleds, a cold wind in our faces, swerving around the corner at the bottom of the hill, and coming to a slow stop on Prospect Street.

"Where are we going?" Eunice asked.

Rosie smiled. "You'll see."

We turned onto Railroad Avenue, which ran downhill and crossed the train tracks. Ahead of us was the flour mill and the little shanties built for the people who worked there. Behind curtained windows, lamps shone, casting rectangles of light on the snow. Some were vacant, their windows and doors boarded up, snow heaped high around them.

"Where are we going?" Eunice asked again.

Without answering, Rosie turned the corner on Hilton Avenue and hopped on her sled to coast downhill. The rest of us followed her.

At the bottom, Rosie stopped. "Here we are," she cried. "The steepest hills in Mount Pleasant!"

With a big grin, she pointed to a massive iron gate decorated with metal leaves and fanciful vines. On it was a sign:

FOREST HEIGHTS CEMETERY

HOURS: EIGHT A.M. TO SUNSET

Of all the places Rosie might have chosen, I hadn't expected the cemetery. It was almost as old as the town itself, which meant the burials went back to the 1700s, and it was built on acres and acres of steep hills. A fence surrounded it, its bars tall and straight, their tops pointed like ancient weapons. *To keep the living out or the dead in?* I wondered.

The moon lit the graves as bright as day, rows and rows of them climbing the hillsides, everything from stone markers for the poor to columns and statues and rows of mausoleums for the rich. So many dead people, more of them than the entire living population of Mount Pleasant, especially now that the flu had taken its terrible toll.

It was the loneliest sight imaginable, a perfect setting for an Edgar Allan Poe story. Jane reached for my hand. We drew close together.

Trying to sound braver than I was, I said, "It's just a

cemetery, Jane." *Just* a cemetery—those tombstones gave me the shivers, but I told myself it was the wind that made me shiver, not the cemetery.

"How are we supposed to get in?" Eunice pointed at a padlock as big as her hand, fastened to the gate with thick chains.

"My brother told me about a place where the bars are bent apart."

Dragging our sleds behind us, we floundered through deep snow. The farther we walked, the more I hoped someone had mended the gap.

Suddenly Rosie stopped. "Here it is, right where Mike said."

The four of us helped her dig away some of the snow. Rosie squeezed through the gap first and maneuvered her sled into the cemetery. Although I had a bad feeling about the cemetery and its occupants, I wasn't about to say I was terrified and run home.

We all followed Rosie through the gap, even Jane, pulling our sleds in after us. Ahead was a steep hill. Tall, thin tombstones climbed upward. At the top was a row of mausoleums, those scary little houses for the dead.

The wind whispered to itself among clumps of firs and cypresses and rattled the branches of tall oak trees. A freight train blew a long warning blast for the Railroad

Avenue crossing. Overhead, the moon gazed down at us with its usual sad look.

Talking loudly, Rosie led the way toward the top, stopping now and then to read a tombstone.

"Here lies Uriah Short," she said. "His life was cut short."

"It doesn't say that!" Lucy pushed her aside to see for herself. "Asleep in the Savior's arms," she corrected Rosie. "That's what it says."

Rosie laughed. "It was a short sleep, though."

Eunice laughed loud enough for all of us.

At the top of the highest hill, we belly flopped on our sleds and shot down, swerving around tombstones and trees. The moon cast inky, sharp-edged shadows. My sled bounced over the snow's icy crust, bucking beneath me like a wild horse. Wind slapped my face with biting cold and snatched my breath away. At any moment I might take to the air and fly over Mount Pleasant as if I rode a magic carpet.

Rosie was the first to coast to a stop at the bottom of the hill. She jumped up from her sled and shouted her joy at the moon.

"Admit it," she cried, "this is the best sledding place in Mount Pleasant, and I found it!"

"Hooray for you," Eunice shouted.

"For she's a jolly good fellow," sang Lucy, "for she's a jolly good fellow, for she's a jolly good fellow, which nobody can deny!"

We all sang another chorus so loudly our voices echoed back from the row of mausoleums above us.

All of us, that is, except Jane. She stood a little apart, brushing snow from her mittens and frowning. "Don't make so much noise," she said.

"Why? "Lucy asked. "Are you scared we'll wake the dead?"

We all laughed except Jane, who said in a low voice, "It's disrespectful."

"Oh, don't be such a scaredy-cat," Eunice said.

Turning her back on Jane, she dragged her sled up the hill behind Lucy and Rosie. I hurried after them. Jane lingered behind, and I waited for her to catch up.

The tombstones on this side of the hill were newer. And plainer. And closer together. Rosie began reading names and dates. The birth dates varied, but the death years were all the same — 1918, 1918, 1918. We were in the part of the cemetery where the flu victims were buried. They stretched out in all directions, uphill, downhill, and sideways.

We stopped in front of a grave guarded by a small

angel. A bouquet of roses frozen black and stiff lay in the snow. The wind blew, and the stems stirred. Their thorns made a faint scritch-scratching sound.

Rosie leaned closer to read the epitaph.

AGNES O'NEIL
BELOVED DAUGHTER OF
EDWARD AND HELEN O'NEIL
BORN SEPTEMBER 3, 1900
DIED OCTOBER 5, 1918
AT REST IN THE ARMS OF THE LORD.

The name was familiar, but I didn't know why until Jane took my arm and whispered, "It's the girl from our first viewing — remember? The one who sang in the choir."

I pictured Agnes as she'd been that day, a pretty girl lying in her coffin, her long hair fanned out on a satin pillow under her head. Now she lay at our feet beneath six feet of earth and four feet of icy hard snow, her eyes closed, waiting to rise from the dead. For a moment, I wondered what she looked like now, but quickly chased the image of a skull from my mind. Mustn't think such things. Bad dreams.

Suddenly fearful, Jane and I backed away, but Rosie ran a mittened hand over the inscription. "Poor Agnes," she said. "It must be dreadful to lie here all alone in the cold."

"Don't speak of it," Eunice whispered. "You're scaring me."

"We came here to sled ride," Lucy said, "not to talk about the dead."

Jane and I followed them up the hill. "Do you think this is where Elsie is buried?" she whispered.

A cold feeling slid up and down my spine. Grabbing Jane's hand, I ran after the others. "Come on, Jane, let's not lag behind."

Out of breath from climbing through knee-deep snow, we rested at the top for a moment. Below us were the lights of the town. I tried to find my house, but it was hard to pick it out. One roof looked much the same as any other. We found our school and the public schools, the churches, the park, and City Hall. We even glimpsed the river, frozen over now, like a wide white highway to the sea.

"Is everybody ready?" Rosie stood with her sled pressed to her chest, all set to get a flying start.

Down we went again, riding the ruts our runners had left the first time. We went faster and faster. My forehead ached with cold, and spray from the sled's runners hit my face. It was bouncier too. Lucy almost hit a tombstone but swerved just in time to topple off her sled into the snow. She lay there laughing, then spread her arms and legs to make an angel.

After three or four, maybe five runs down the hill, Rosie said, "I've got an idea. Let's hook our sleds together and go down in a train."

Rosie was first, of course. Lucy was second, then Eunice, then Jane, and I was last of all, the caboose, the best position to whip back and forth behind the others. Rosie gave the command, and we pushed off, picking up speed as we raced down the hill.

I slid from one side to the other, almost colliding with Rosie more than once. Halfway down, my sled broke away from the others, and I found myself hurtling downhill sideways with no control over speed or direction. My wild ride ended with a jolt that sent me flying through the air. I hit something and everything went black.

When I opened my eyes, I was sprawled on my face, at the feet of an angel. For a moment, I thought I was dead and the angel had brought me to heaven, a cold, snowy place filled with pain, but then Jane's voice broke through the darkness.

"Annie, Annie, are you all right?" The other girls had gathered around me. It made me dizzy to look at them.

Their voices hurt my ears, and my head rang with noise that made it hard to hard to understand what they were saying.

I didn't know if I was all right or about to die. My head hurt so fiercely I thought it must be broken like Jack's in the nursery rhyme. I was afraid to move in case I couldn't.

"You were knocked clean out," Rosie said. "You hit that angel, and bam!"

"It's a mercy you weren't killed," Jane whispered.

"Look at me," Lucy said. She held up her hand. "How many fingers can you see?"

I squinted hard, but my head was still spinning, and I could barely see her hand, let alone her fingers.

"What's your name?"

"You know my name."

"Say it anyway."

I said my name and told her my age and where I lived, but I simply could not count those fingers. Or tell her who was president.

"We need to take her to my house," Lucy said. "Look at all the blood she's lost. And she might have a concussion. You can die hours after it happens."

Everyone looked at my blood, including me. It had run across the snow and puddled in a hole it melted. Some of it was red, and some was pink from the melted snow, but it seemed like a huge amount to have come out of me. In fact, I thought I might faint just seeing it there. I touched my face, and my mitten came away red. No wonder I couldn't see Lucy's fingers. I had blood in my eyes.

"We'll get in so much trouble if we take Annie to your house," Eunice said.

"No, we won't," Rosie said. "We'll tell Dr. Hughes Annie hit the stone wall at the bottom of High Street. We'll never ever say anything to anyone about the cemetery."

"Like when we had the fight with Elsie?" Eunice asked. "And we made a solemn oath not to tell?"

"Yes, exactly like that."

"Do we have to spit on our hands?" Lucy asked.

"Not this time," Rosie said. "Just swear to say nothing. It's too cold to take our mittens off."

My head ached and throbbed and pounded, but with Jane's help, I managed to stand up. I saw two of everyone. They multiplied into triplets, quintuplets, as distorted as reflections in fun house mirrors. Then the snow and the tombstones began to spin faster and faster. I grabbed Jane's arm, and she stopped me from falling,

"Can you walk?" Jane asked.

"I think so." But after I took a step, I sat down. Lucy muttered something I couldn't understand. "What did you say?" I asked her.

"Me?" Lucy shook her head. "I didn't say anything."

"Well, somebody's mumbling." I looked around. "Can't you hear it? It's really loud. It's making my ears buzz."

They stood there staring at me. None of them would admit to saying a word or hearing anything.

"You must have a concussion," Lucy said. "Help me get her on a sled, Rosie. She needs to see my father. And soon!"

Since my sled was damaged, Rosie and Jane made me lie on Rosie's. It belonged to her brother Mike and was longer than anyone else's. I didn't argue. I was too dizzy to walk, everything was still blurry, and my head echoed with mumbles and mutters that sounded like someone talking in foreign languages. I was scared my brain was ruined and I'd be dead by morning. In a few days, I'd be sleeping here in the cemetery.

Rosie and Jane pulled me slowly through the snow, trying not to bounce me around too much or bump any tombstones. I heard Eunice say she was glad we were going home. She was cold, and she really didn't like the cemetery very much. Lucy said she'd been having a swell time and wished I hadn't ruined all the fun by crashing into that stupid angel.

All the while, the voice only I heard mumbled and muttered and shrieked until I thought I'd lose my mind.

ELEVEN

IT WAS A LONG, cold sled ride to Lucy's house. Every bump hurt, but as we left the cemetery behind, the awful mumbling and muttering voices slowly faded away, and I began to feel better. Still weak, still dizzy when I lifted my head, but I believed I might live after all.

Lucy ran up her porch steps and called her father to come outside and carry me into the house. Dr. Hughes took one look at my bloody head and carried me through the warm house, straight to his office. Laying me on an examining table, he cleaned away the blood and examined the cut.

"It's not a fatal wound," he said with a smile, "but you'll need a few stitches. Even superficial scalp cuts bleed excessively, and this one is fairly deep."

He paused and shone a little light in my eyes. "I'm

concerned about the possibility of a concussion. Can you tell me exactly what happened?"

I said I wasn't sure, so Rosie explained. "We were sled riding on High Street," she said, "and Annie crashed into the stone wall at the bottom where Henry got killed last year. She knocked herself out, and she was bleeding all over the snow, and we thought she was dead like Henry, and we were so scared—"

I don't know how long Rosie would have gone on embellishing the story if Lucy hadn't interrupted.

"She knew her name, but she couldn't count my fingers and she said she heard voices in her head," Lucy told her father. "She was so dizzy she couldn't sit up at first, she just lay in the snow. When she did get up, she couldn't walk straight."

Dr. Hughes held his hand up in front of my face and peered into my eyes. "How many fingers do you see?"

His hand was blurry, a blob. I couldn't focus on it. Unsure, I hesitated and squinted. "Four?" I guessed.

He shook his head. "Try again." I failed once more, twice more.

"It's a concussion all right," he said. "Blurred vision is a symptom."

He looked at me closely. "Are you dizzy?"

I nodded and my head throbbed with pain.

"Nausea?"

"Yes," I whispered.

"How about your ears? Any ringing or buzzing?"

I whispered yes again.

By now I was expecting to be sent to the hospital. My head hurt so bad I could scarcely hold it up. My stomach threatened to empty itself right there and then on Dr. Hughes's shoes. I struggled not to cry.

Dr. Hughes patted my shoulder. "You'll need to rest for a few days. By next week, you'll feel fine."

Turning toward the door, he said, "I'm going to call your parents now and ask their permission to stitch you up. I'm sure they'll be here any moment."

To Jane, Rosie, and Eunice he said, "As soon as I have Annie sorted, I'll drive you girls home."

After Dr. Hughes left, Eunice gave me a pitying look. "Oooh, stitches," she said, "I had my chin sewn up when I was little, and it really hurt. I still have the scar. See?"

She pointed at a faint white line I'd never even noticed and winced.

Lucy frowned at Eunice. "You can make a bet my father didn't do that." To me she said, "Don't worry, Annie, my father won't hurt you, and you won't have a scar. People say he's the best stitcher in Mount Pleasant."

Dr. Hughes returned and told Lucy and the others to

leave the room. Before I knew it, he had my cut stitched up and my head bandaged.

Like Lucy said, it hadn't hurt much at all—just prick, prick, and he was done. The worst part was when he shaved a circle on my scalp about the size of a silver dollar. He said my hair would grow back in no time and no one would be the wiser. I hoped he was right, but I was certain I'd have a permanent bald spot. People would point and laugh. The boys would call me Baldy.

Mother and Father arrived just as Dr. Hughes was finishing up. You never saw such a scene, Mother fussing over me and Father asking how it happened until I felt so dizzy I almost fainted. That silenced them.

"Annie needs to rest," Dr. Hughes told them. "Put her to bed, cover her with warm blankets, and sit beside her. She has a concussion and needs watching all night."

Mother was all aflutter again. Father seemed torn between comforting her and comforting me and tried to do both, turning to her and then me and then back to her.

"Keep Annie in bed for a few days," Dr. Hughes said. "Check on her frequently. I'll visit tomorrow afternoon about four, if that's convenient."

While the doctor gave Mother more instructions, Father wrapped me up in the blanket he'd brought and carried me to the car.

As he settled me in the back seat, he asked again how it had happened.

"Father, please," I whispered, "I don't remember much, and I'm tired and I want to go home."

"Yes, yes, of course, Annie." He went to fetch Mother, and soon the three of us were driving through the snowy streets. Feeling as if I were sinking down, down, down into snow, deep snow, cold snow, I fell into a troubled sleep. Suddenly I was in the cemetery again, flying through the air, crashing into the angel, only she was made of snow and she broke into pieces when I hit her. And a girl as white as snow stood where the angel had been, and she was wearing a flu mask.

Even though the mask hid her face, I knew who she was, but I couldn't remember her name. She took my hand and held it in hers, a grip as hard and cold as ice. It felt as if our hands had frozen together. I'd never escape, she'd never let me go. And then she pulled me down into the snow, deeper and deeper, and I saw a door, tall and black, and knew she meant to leave me there — at death's door.

Cold air hit my face, and I woke with a cry. The car door was open. Father leaned over me. "Wake up, Annie. We're home."

As he lifted me, I wrapped my arms tightly around his

neck, feeling the warmth of his body through his heavy wool coat. Like a child, I pressed my face against his shoulder.

"Were you dreaming?" Mother asked. "You sounded scared."

Without raising my head, I whispered "Yes," but I didn't tell her what had frightened me.

Father carried me up to bed. My lamp glowed with a soft warm light, illuminating a shelf of books, the toys above them, the dollhouse in the corner, the rocking chair, the roses on the wallpaper, the lacy curtains shutting out the night. Never had my room looked so comforting, so safe. My old bear lay on my pillow, waiting to comfort me.

Mother undressed me and helped me into a warm flannel nightgown. Then she covered me with so many blankets I thought I might suffocate. She tucked the bear under the covers and I hugged him.

"Father and I will take turns sitting with you tonight," Mother said. "If you need anything, just tell us."

Even though I was exhausted, I slept badly, waking from dreams of the cemetery and the snow angel. The masked girl dragged me down to the black door over and over again, but I always woke up before it opened. If I stayed asleep, I knew the door would open and I would die.

At last the long night passed. Mother brought me breakfast on a tray — a soft-boiled egg in a little yellow cup shaped like a baby chick, toast, and weak tea. She'd cut the toast into little strips we called soldiers. I dipped them into my egg just as I had when I was little.

"How does your head feel?" she asked.

"It hurts," I said.

She went downstairs and returned with a spoonful of aspirin she'd mashed into grape jelly to hide its bitter taste.

Father came in to give me a hug and then left for work. I heard the car engine start with a sputter then a *putt-putt-putt*ing as he drove away.

Mother sat in the rocker, dividing her time between knitting and reading to me. She'd finished the blue sweater and was working on a beret to go with it. The click of the needles was relaxing, and the sound of her voice comforted me. I'd never read *The Swiss Family Robinson*. The story of a family marooned on an island took my mind off my bad dreams and stilled the mumble and mutter of voices in my aching head.

Dr. Hughes looked in on me as he'd promised. He pronounced me in good health and coming along as well as could be expected. Since my head still ached fiercely and I was dizzy, forgetful, and weak, he told Mother to keep me in bed for at least a few more days, maybe longer.

That night I slept better, waking only twice from the dream. In the afternoon Jane came to see me. We played a few games of old maid and a round of checkers, but I couldn't keep my mind on my kings, so we put the board aside.

She told me another classmate, Hester Grimes, had come down with the flu but was already on the mend.

"No one has died in Baltimore for three whole days," Jane said. "I read it in the paper."

"That's good. I hope it's soon gone forever."

We talked for a while about school. The girls had begun rehearsing for the spring program, and Miss Harrison had chosen Jane to recite Longfellow's poem "The Wreck of the Hesperus."

"It's very sad," she said.

"It's also very long," I said.

"Well, Miss Harrison said I needn't memorize the whole poem. She wants me to tell what it's about and recite what she calls 'selected stanzas.'"

"In other words, just the saddest parts."

"Yes, the ones about the captain's little daughter and the shipwreck and how she freezes to death in the ocean and a fisherman finds her lashed to the mast. I already know the end by heart." Jane cleared her throat and recited:

> *The salt sea was frozen on her breast,*
> *The salt tears in her eyes;*

And he saw her hair, like the brown sea-weed,
   On the billows fall and rise.

Such was the wreck of the Hesperus,
   In the midnight and the snow!
Christ save us all from a death like this,
   On the reef of Norman's Woe!

Jane had a perfect face for the poem, sorrowful and pale, and she got teary eyed as she spoke.

"I hope I don't cry at the recital," Jane said. "But it's just so sad, especially after the flu and the people we know who died, not at sea of course, but right here in Mount Pleasant. The man and woman across my street; Arthur Livingston, the boy on my corner; and I don't know how many others." She paused. "Oh, and poor Elsie. I'll feel bad about her my whole life."

An image of the masked girl in the snowy cemetery arose in my mind, and I closed my eyes for a moment. I longed to tell Jane about my dream. Maybe she'd understand what it meant. But talking about it might make it stronger.

Jane looked at me as if she were worried about me. "Miss Harrison wants to know if I should bring your assignments so you can keep up with the class."

"Not yet." I slid down in bed. "It hurts my head my head to think. And I get so tired. All I want to do is sleep."

Jane stood up. "Oh dear, Annie, you need to rest, and here I am keeping you awake with idle chatter."

"Can you come back tomorrow?"

"Yes, of course. Should I bring Rosie or —"

"No, not yet. Just you." Truthfully, I didn't have enough energy to cope with Rosie, who'd no doubt bounce on the bed and tell jokes and talk too loud.

At the end of seven long days, Dr. Hughes came to remove the stitches in my head. After checking me over, he told Mother I needed to build up my strength. He recommended fresh air and limited exercise. A good walk, for instance, would do me a world of good.

When Mother asked about school, he suggested waiting until next week. "Let's get Annie back on her feet and worry about school later."

That was fine with me. I was in no hurry to sit in a desk all day and listen to Miss Harrison. I tired easily, my mind still drifted, my head still hurt (though not nearly as badly), and the voices still muttered.

After I'd been up and about for a few days, Mother asked if I'd be all right on my own. "It's bridge day at the women's club," she said, "and Irene Hughes is begging me to come. Last week she had a terrible partner and did very poorly." Mother stroked my forehead. "Irene says Lucy misses you and hopes you feel better soon."

"I'll be fine by myself," I told her. "I'll spend the afternoon reading the mystery you brought home from the library."

Mother smiled and ran upstairs to powder her nose, as she put it, and I curled up on the sofa with *The Moonstone*. Jane told me it was too scary for her, but, scary or not, I knew I'd like it. I'd read *The Woman in White* and loved it — *The Moonstone* couldn't be any scarier than that.

After Mother left, the house was very quiet. The *tick-tock-tick* of the clock on the mantel was the loudest sound. That and the occasional scratching and tapping of branches at the window.

I'd no sooner begun reading than I found myself thinking about my dream. Last night it had been so vivid. As usual, I lay at the angel's feet, bleeding in the snow. The girl with the mask emerged and stood above me. As she dragged me down into the dark, I almost recognized her. I awoke with her name on my lips, but it slipped away and I shivered with fear.

Suddenly I felt an irresistible urge to return to the cemetery. Maybe if I saw the angel again, I could banish it from my dreams. Tossing off the afghan, I pulled on the blue sweater Mother had knitted for me and bundled up in my coat, snow pants, scarf, hat, and mittens. I looked as round as a snowman, but even though it was the beginning of February, the weather was still cold. We'd had snow the day before, and it lay atop the dirty old snow in a fresh white coat, as if someone had painted it there to hide the ugliness beneath.

It was a long walk. By the time I came to the shanties where the millworkers lived, I was cold and tired. My head throbbed, and I wondered if I'd overdone the limited exercise Dr. Hughes had prescribed for me.

This time the gates were open. A horse-drawn hearse passed me, followed by a line of black carriages. As the funeral procession slowly disappeared into the depths of the cemetery, I crossed my fingers inside my mittens, a habit I'd gotten into whenever I saw a hearse — a sort of protection against the flu. So far it had worked.

I considered walking up the plowed driveway, much easier than wading through deep snow, but I wasn't sure I'd find the angel without following the exact route we'd taken that night.

I trudged along the fence until I found the gap. Wiggling through, I looked for the tracks we'd made, but new snow covered them. I should have given up then and turned back, but instead I began climbing the hill. It was steeper than I remembered, and I rested for a while at the top.

Seven crows flew out of a nearby grove of oak trees and passed in a ragged black line over my head. I thought of the old counting rhyme which began *one crow for sorrow,* but what did seven crows mean? I'd forgotten.

Slowly and carefully, I made my way downhill. My boots filled with snow, and my cold toes tingled with pain. My head throbbed, and my skull echoed with mumbling muttering sounds. The bright sun on the white snow blinded me. Unable to see properly, I fell and slid to the bottom, landing at the feet of a stone angel.

Near me, a splintered bit of my sled poked up through the snow. I'd come to the right place.

But the noise in my head was so loud and hurt so much that I lay where I'd fallen and looked up at the angel. She was smaller than I remembered, no bigger than a doll, but she had a mean expression, not what you'd expect on an angel's face at all. From her outstretched finger, a flu mask dangled, twisting in the wind.

Frightened by the mask, I squinted at the inscription beneath the angel's stone-cold toes. The words were blurred by a frosting of frozen snow. Carefully I brushed it aside and read

HERE LIES ELSIE SCHNEIDER
BELOVED DAUGHTER OF
HILDA AND KARL SCHNEIDER
BORN 15 MARCH 1906
DIED 8 NOVEMBER 1918
IN HER TWELFTH YEAR

In a panic of fear and guilt, I scrambled to my feet and backed away, slipping and sliding on the icy snow, breaking through the crust and sinking deeper with every effort I made to run. Of all the graves in the cemetery, I'd crashed into Elsie's.

TWELVE

AS I STRUGGLED IN THE SNOW, the voices in my head became one voice, and it was speaking words in a language I understood.

"Hello, Annie Browne," the voice said. "At last you've come."

Elsie floated above the snow. She was deathly pale and not quite solid. Her lusterless blond hair blew around her face, and she wore the same pale blue silk dress and matching bow she'd worn when I last saw her lying in her coffin, apparently as dead as dead can be.

"Why don't you say hello?" she asked. "Surely you haven't forgotten me already."

She drifted closer. Her bare feet grazed the snow's

surface but left no tracks. I wanted to turn my head away, but I couldn't help looking at her. I saw her crooked teeth, longer and more yellow than I remembered. Her skin was stretched tight over her skull, and her eyes gleamed in their sockets. She looked as if she wanted to take my life and make it hers.

Elsie laughed. "Well, I do declare," she said. "You're afraid of me. I wonder why? Could it be you think I want to get even with you?"

Desperately I looked for someone to rescue me, but the only living creature in sight was a crow, hunched on a nearby stone cross and watching me.

"One crow for sorrow," Elsie whispered in a voice as harsh as the wind on a winter night. "*Your* sorrow."

I finally found my voice. "You're not real, you can't be, you're dead, I saw you in your coffin. I saw them take you away in a hearse. They *buried* you." I pointed at her grave. "Right there — can't you see your name written at the angel's feet?"

Elsie ran one finger over the inscription. "I'd still be sleeping if you hadn't waked me up crashing into my grave. You disturbed some of the others as well. You must have heard us complaining."

"I didn't know, Elsie, I couldn't understand the voices, I thought it was just noise in my head." *This can't be true,* I thought. *I must be dreaming. I'll open my eyes and find my-self at home on the sofa.*

Elsie flashed her terrible teeth in a smile. "But you understand me now, don't you?"

"What do you want from me?"

"You know what I want."

"No, I don't, I swear I don't." I hid my face behind my hands to keep from looking into her eyes.

"Now that I'm dead, I mean to have the friend I wanted when I was alive — *you,* Annie."

"How can we be friends? You're, you're —"

As I fumbled for the right words, Elsie shrugged. "Oh, yes, you're right. I'm dead. Well, la tee dah, we can't let a little thing like that come between us, can we?"

"I didn't want to be your friend when you were alive, and I don't want to be your friend now." I stared at Elsie. "I have plenty of friends already!"

"Not for long," Elsie said. "Soon everyone will hate you even more than they hated me."

"My friends won't turn against me. Not ever!"

"Just wait," Elsie said. "You'll see."

A gang of crows settled themselves noisily in a tall oak. Elsie turned away to count them. "Seven," she said. "Do you know what seven crows mean?"

When I shook my head, she said, *"Seven crows for a*

secret, never to be told. That's what our friendship will be — a secret never to be told." She laughed. "Even if you tell, no one will believe you."

The sun was low in the sky now, and the tombstone's blue shadows were long and menacing. The wind blew harder, and I thought I might freeze to death in the cemetery.

"Please let me go home, Elsie," I begged.

"First you have to promise something." Plucking the flu mask from the angel's stone finger, she thrust it at me. "I think Rosie should have this, don't you?"

"No." I put my hands behind my back. "Get that thing away from me. I won't touch it!"

Elsie blew her cold breath in my face. "You always do what Rosie says. Now you must do what *I* say."

"What if I don't?"

"Do you want to go home?" She held out the mask. "Or do you want to stay here and freeze to death?"

With revulsion, I took it from her. "What am I supposed to do with this?"

"When you go back to school, put the mask in Rosie's bookbag. Don't let anyone see you." She paused to be sure I was listening. "All the things we do will be secrets. I'll know if you tell."

With that, Elsie faded away, and I was alone with the

seven crows. They sat on a branch with their heads turned toward me. How long and sharp their beaks were, how beady their eyes. How wicked they looked.

Stuffing the mask into my pocket, I pulled free of the snow's grip. My legs and feet were numb with cold and weak with fear. Without giving my sled a thought, I stumbled downhill to the fence and squeezed through the gap in the railings. Behind me the crows cawed. Their voices sounded like laughter.

As I hurried past the shabby little houses on Railroad Avenue, I told myself Elsie had been a hallucination brought on by my concussion. I wasn't over it yet — it must be worse than Dr. Hughes thought.

But how was I to explain the flu mask in my pocket? I pulled it out and looked at it. Dingy and tattered, it was disgusting. I wanted to throw it away, but Elsie's voice rang in my head. She'd know if I didn't put it in Rosie's bookbag. *She'd know.*

But why did she want me to put it there? Would Rosie get the flu? Was that Elsie's intention?

I wadded the mask up and threw it into a pile of snow left by the plow. Before I'd taken more than ten steps, I turned around and went back for it. She'd know, she'd know, I knew she'd know. And she'd make something horrible happen.

By the time I reached my house, I was gasping for breath. Elsie's words spun in my brain as sharp as knives and just as painful—*best friends forever, you and me, me and you, no one else, you and me, me and you, best friends . . .*

No, no, no—it couldn't be, mustn't be. There had to be a way to escape from Elsie. But how? She might be following me at this very moment, cloaked in darkness, invisible but always there, just behind me. I looked back, fearing I'd see her, but the sidewalk was empty.

I opened the front door and ran inside, straight into Mother's arms. "Where have you been?" she cried. "It's almost dark."

She drew back and studied my face. "Look at you, you're as white as a ghost. What's wrong? What's happened?"

"Oh, Mother, Mother," I sobbed, "please don't be upset. I'm sorry I'm late. I was at the library, and I lost track of the time. I ran all the way home."

"You must be exhausted," Mother said. "Let me help you with your boots and snow pants. Then you can change your clothes and rest by the fire. I'll bring you a nice hot cup of tea."

Soon I was lying on the couch covered with one of Mother's hand-knit afghans. The tea was hot and the fire warm. My cold feet and hands gradually thawed.

"You've overexerted yourself." Mother looked worried. "Dr. Hughes said moderate exercise, not a ten-block walk to the library."

I finished my tea and set the cup and saucer on a low table beside the couch. The firelight shone through the fragile porcelain. Just as I began to relax, I sensed a movement in the dark corner behind Father's chair. I waited for it to move again. Had Elsie followed me home and slipped through the door behind me?

The shadows moved again. When I leaned forward to see better, Mother looked at me. "Why are you staring into the corner, Annie? Is something there?"

"No, no, of course not." I leaned back against a sofa pillow and forced myself to gaze into the fire. I wouldn't look in the corner. I wouldn't. And I would not, would not, would not put the flu mask in Rosie's bookbag. Elsie wasn't real, she was a hallucination, and so was the mask. If I looked in my coat pocket, it wouldn't be there.

"You seem worried," Mother said. "Does your head hurt?"

"No, my head's fine, but I was wondering about something. May I ask you a silly question?"

"You may ask anything you want."

I hesitated a moment, afraid of what Mother might say. "Do you believe in ghosts?"

"Ghosts?" She looked startled. "Good heavens, no. Why do you ask?"

"Oh, I was reading a book about ghosts at the library — true stories that really happened to people."

"True? I doubt that very much."

"Well," I said slowly, "one of the stories was about a girl who died, and her ghost came back to haunt a girl who'd been mean to her when the ghost was alive. The ghost said she was the girl's best friend and the girl had to do everything she told her to do, no matter how bad it was. And the girl had to keep it secret."

"No wonder you're upset. That sounds very scary." Mother finished the row she was knitting and looked at me. "What happened to the girl?"

"The library closed, and I didn't have time to finish reading the story."

Mother smiled and resumed knitting. "Don't worry, Annie. The person who told that story made it up. In real life, things like that don't happen."

Oh, Mother, Mother, I wish I could tell you how wrong you are.

THIRTEEN

MONDAY MORNING came long before I was ready for it. I dressed in my uniform, and Mother helped me tie my hair ribbon.

"You look so pretty," she told me. "Everyone in your class will be very happy to see you."

I gazed into the mirror and pointed to the bald spot, smaller now but still visible, as was the jagged red line of the scar running through it. "What about this?"

Mother smiled. "Think of it as your red badge of courage," she said. "All the girls will want to hear about your accident."

Just as I finished my oatmeal, Jane knocked at the door.

When I ran to meet her, she gave me a big hug. "Oh,

I'm so glad you're well enough to come to school, Annie. I've missed you so much."

"I've missed you, too."

As Jane walked beside me chattering about the spring program, I felt stiff and uncomfortable and found little to say. My bookbag's strap weighed heavily on my shoulder, and all I thought about was the mask hidden at the bottom.

As we climbed the school steps, I saw Elsie sitting on a ledge above the door. She swung her bare feet and waved at me. "Don't forget to do what I told you — I'll know if you don't do it."

She vanished as quickly as she'd appeared, but after Jane and I went inside, Elsie joined us, so close I felt the cold of her body through my coat.

"Best friends, best friends," she whispered in my ear.

"Go away, I'm not your friend!" I shouted. "Leave me alone!"

Jane turned to me in alarm. "What do you mean, Annie? Of course you're my friend. Why did you say that?"

"I wasn't talking to you," I said, but my voice was wrong. I meant to sound sorry, but I sounded mad instead.

"But there's no one here but me," Jane said.

Elsie blew cold air in her face and laughed when Jane shivered.

"You gave me a headache talking and talking and

talking about 'The Wreck of the Hesperus,'" I said. "It's a boring poem, and I'm sick of it."

I stared at Jane, horrified at myself. Why had I said such a dreadful thing? It was as if the words had tumbled out of my mouth without my meaning to say them. Yet I couldn't find it in me to apologize.

"Are you mad at me?" Jane asked.

"Let's just say I'm tired of your whiny voice."

I wanted to take back what I'd said, what Elsie had *made* me say, but instead I walked away from Jane, into the cloakroom, where we hung our coats. Rosie's bookbag, emptied of everything but her lunch, lay on the floor beside her boots. Elsie perched on a windowsill and watched me.

Without looking at me, Jane hung up her coat, pulled off her boots, snow pants, mittens, and hat, and went into the classroom.

I hurried after her, hoping to make up, but Miss Harrison stopped me with a hug. "I'm so glad you're back, Annie. We missed you."

I opened my mouth to tell her how much I'd missed her, but Elsie spoke for me. "I didn't miss you or anyone else," I heard myself say. "I hate this school and everyone in it."

Miss Harrison looked at me as if I'd slapped her. "Annie Browne," she said, "I've never heard you talk like that.

Perhaps you'd better march yourself back into the cloak-room and stay there until I give you permission to join the class."

I shrugged and walked away, my head high to show her I wasn't sorry and I didn't care. The room was very quiet. Though I didn't look at anyone, I knew the other girls were staring at me. The silence rang with shock and dismay. What was wrong with Annie Browne?

Alone except for Elsie, I found myself removing the flu mask from my bookbag and tucking it into Rosie's. I didn't want to do it, but I couldn't stop. It was as if I were outside my own body, watching myself.

On the windowsill, Elsie clapped her hands. "You are now my true friend."

In the classroom, the girls recited the Pledge of Allegiance and the Lord's Prayer. Their voices rose and fell in unison. Elsie had made me into an outsider again.

Elsie hovered in front of me, her face close to mine. "See? Soon everyone will hate you," she jeered, "just the way they hated me."

I tried to back away, but my shoulders touched the coats hanging from their hooks. I was trapped just inches from her, close enough to see every pore in her pale skin, close enough to smell her earthy odor.

"But you'll have me," she whispered, "you'll always

have me, your best friend, your bosom buddy, as they say in those dumb girls' stories I used to read."

"I'd rather have nobody."

She floated above me singing, "I ain't got no body, and nobody cares about me."

"Go away," I shouted. "I hate you!"

Miss Harrison appeared in the cloakroom doorway. "What are you shouting about, Annie? Haven't you behaved badly enough for one day?"

Behind her, my classmates spun around to look, their eyes wide.

I reached out to Miss Harrison. Tears ran down my face, but I couldn't speak because my head was spinning and so was the room. I felt as if were being sucked into a well of darkness. No one was there except Elsie, watching me eagerly.

When I opened my eyes, I was lying on a cot in the health room. Elsie perched on a chair beside me, obviously pleased to see me in trouble.

Nurse Evans leaned over me, her forehead creased into worry lines.

"Do you know where you are, Annie?'

"I'm in the health room."

"Do you remember what you were doing before you fainted?"

I shook my head. "I took off my coat and my boots, my snow pants, mittens, hat, scarf . . ." I let my voice sink low and trail off.

"Do you remember being mean to Jane and sassy to Miss Harrison?"

I widened my eyes. "Why would I be mean to Jane? She's my best friend. I'd never be rude to Miss Harrison. She's my favorite teacher."

While I stumbled through my denials, I felt Elsie pinch me. "I'm your best friend now," she hissed. "And don't forget it."

Without thinking, I said out loud, "Go away and leave me alone!"

Nurse Evans stared at me, shocked. "I'm calling your mother," she said. "I think you've come back to school too soon. A concussion often makes people irritable. They say things they don't mean; they aren't themselves."

I tried to sit up, but Nurse Evans said, "Lie still, Annie, and rest. Your mother will be here soon."

The moment Elsie and I were alone, I said, "You think you're so clever, but I'll never let you in my head again."

Elsie smiled. "Too late, Annie. I'm already in your head — and I don't plan to leave."

From a corner, she watched me through narrowed eyes. I tried to stare back, but I couldn't bear looking at her.

Nurse Evans stood just outside the door, explaining my behavior to Miss Harrison.

"Oh, poor dear Annie," Miss Harrison said. "I knew there must be reason. I'll talk to Jane. She's heartbroken."

Elsie sniffed. "Jane hasn't seen anything yet."

I stared at the water stain on the health room ceiling and tried to make its shape into something interesting — anything to avoid thinking about Elsie. A face maybe. I studied it more closely and realized it looked like Elsie. Shutting my eyes, I waited for Mother to arrive.

On the way home, Mother took me to see Dr. Hughes. He spent a lot of time shining lights in my eyes and asking questions. When the exam was over, he said, "I don't detect any signs of damage or lingering effects. Perhaps you simply need more rest."

Mother told him about my visit to the library and the state I was in when I came home.

"That must be it. No more long walks until you feel like yourself."

"Should we keep her home from school for a few days?" Mother asked.

"No, no, that won't be necessary," Dr. Hughes said. "Annie's missed so much school already. We don't want her to fall behind in her studies."

• • •

While he and Mother chatted, I looked for Elsie. I finally spotted her in a shadowy corner. She was studying a chart of the human skeleton as if she were looking into a mirror.

Dr. Hughes's eyes followed mine to the spot where Elsie floated.

"What are you looking at, Annie? You've been gazing around the room as if you expect to see something."

"There's a cobweb in the corner." I pointed. "Right there. That's what I was looking at."

Mother squinted at the ceiling. "I don't see a cobweb or even a speck of dust, Annie, and even if I did, I certainly wouldn't mention it. It's impolite to find fault."

Dr. Hughes laughed. "I think our Annie was just being helpful."

Mother handed me my coat and all the other things I had to wear in cold weather. While I put them on, I felt her watching me closely. Elsie watched, too.

As we walked down Portman Street toward home, Mother took my hand in hers as if I were five years old again. "Annie," she said, "are you certain you're all right?"

"Dr. Hughes thinks so."

Elsie was walking just ahead, barefoot, wearing nothing but her silk dress. Every now and then she floated about five feet off the ground and circled Mother and me.

"My," Mother said, "how much colder it feels in this spot. It must be the shadow of the pine trees."

Elsie grinned at me and made a face at Mother, who walked on, complaining about the cold.

At home, Elsie followed me upstairs and prowled around my room. Nodding to herself, she touched my dollhouse, my books, my bed, the lacy curtains. She opened the wardrobe and examined my clothes. She scooped up Edward Bear and made him growl.

"Yes, it's all just as it was the time I visited," she murmured, "the one day in my whole life I had a friend."

Smirking at me, she picked up Antoinette, freshly mended and looking as perfect as the day I found her under the Christmas tree. Tipping the doll back and forth, she watched her eyes open and shut and listened to her cry "Mama, Mama."

I reached for Antoinette, but Elsie tossed her aside. "You have everything I ever wanted. All I wanted was for you to share it with me. But, oh no, you were too selfish."

The more Elsie talked, the angrier she got. "I needed you to be my friend. Was that too much to ask?"

"If you wanted me to be your friend, you shouldn't have broken my favorite doll. You tried to make the other girls hate me. You wouldn't let me play games or seesaw —"

"Oh, pish posh," Elsie said. "You never gave me a chance to be nice. You shut me out of everything. You and those other girls. Why did you like them better than me? What was so special about them?"

"Annie," Mother called from downstairs, "is someone up there with you?"

I left my room and scurried down the steps. "No," I lied. "Nobody's upstairs. I'm by myself."

"It sounded as if you were talking to someone."

I shook my head. "I was just playing with my doll-house."

Elsie floated down the stairs and blew cold air down Mother's neck.

Mother shivered. "The house is so drafty tonight."

Elsie paused at the front door. "Ta-ta, Annie. See you soon." Grinning her terrible grin, she passed through the door as if it weren't there.

"Don't come back," I muttered in a voice too low for Mother to hear.

The next morning, Jane came to fetch me just as she had yesterday, but there was no hug this time, not even a smile. She looked as if she feared I might snap at her again.

Perched atop a street sign on the corner, Elsie waved to me. While we waited to cross the street, Jane asked me what I was looking at.

"Nothing, nothing at all." I raised my voice so Elsie would be sure to hear.

"Why are you shouting?" Jane asked. "Are you still mad at me?"

"Stop asking so many questions, Jane. It's annoying."

Jane studied my face. "Miss Harrison says you're acting this way because of the concussion. It's making you cross."

"You'd make anybody cross!" I'd done it again. Elsie was in my head making me say things I didn't mean.

"Well, pardon me." Jane ran across the street and up the school steps. When I caught up with her in the cloakroom, she wouldn't look at me. She'd been crying.

I wanted to apologize, but Elsie pinched me. "Who's your best friend now, Annie?" she asked.

I glared at Elsie. "You'll never be my best friend."

"And I'll never be your best friend," Jane said, and left the cloakroom.

I wanted to run after her and explain I hadn't been talking to her — but how would that sound? As far as Jane knew, she and I had been alone in the cloakroom.

Without saying anything, I went through the morning drill with the others. Roll call, Pledge of Allegiance, Lord's Prayer. When we sat down, I saw Elsie's flu mask on Miss Harrison's desk. My stomach lurched, and I covered my mouth in fear I might vomit.

Miss Harrison held up the mask, holding it by two fingers as if she were displaying a dead mouse. "Rosie found this in her bookbag after school yesterday."

Everyone stared at Rosie. From the tense way she sat, I knew the mask had frightened her.

Elsie smiled at me from the windowsill. Her desk was gone, so she no longer had a place behind me. I was the last one in my row.

"Rosie and I agree that someone in this room put the mask in her bag. I'd like that person to raise her hand and admit her guilt. I'd also like her to explain why she put it there. I don't believe influenza germs survive in cold weather, but suppose they do? Suppose Rosie comes down with flu?"

The class sat so still I could hear the girl beside me breathing. The radiator hissed. Someone dropped a pencil. But no one raised a hand.

"Girls," Miss Harrison said, "this is serious. It will not be taken lightly. Which one of you put the mask in Rosie's bookbag?"

She looked up and down the rows of desks, staring hard at each of us. With clasped hands, I forced myself to meet her eyes, to look innocent. Annie Browne could not possibly have done such a thing. But her gaze lingered on me.

Miss Harrison sighed. "I expect a written confession

to be placed on my desk by the end of the day. If it does not appear, you will all remain after school until the guilty person identifies herself. Now, open your geography books to chapter ten, page fifty-five."

At ten, we were released for recess. Elsie floated behind me as I crossed the snowy playground. My friends huddled together by the swings. When they saw me, they didn't smile or even say hello.

Rosie walked up to me. "You put the mask in my bag, didn't you?"

I backed away, frightened by her anger. "Of course not. Why would I do something like that?"

"You were in the cloakroom all by yourself. It had to be you, Annie."

The other girls, the whole class, actually, drew in around us.

"I didn't do it," I cried. "I swear I didn't." I was aware of Elsie sitting in one of the playground swings, her bare feet dangling as she pumped herself higher, a smug expression on her face.

"Did so," someone shouted. "Did so!"

The first snowball hit me. Then another, then a fusillade. Scared of their anger, I turned and ran. They chased me, throwing more snowballs and screaming, "Did so, did so!"

The snowballs were hard, as if they'd been packed with ice. They hit my head, my neck, my back, my legs. I couldn't escape. It was like being chased by a pack of wild dogs. I started crying. How could this be happening? Elsie was dead, but she was still ruining my life. Just as she'd predicted, my friends had turned against me. Now I was the one everyone hated.

Finally Miss Harrison appeared at the school door. The girls dropped their snowballs and stood still.

In the background, Elsie swung higher and higher. No one noticed the swing moving but me.

"What is the meaning of this behavior, girls?" Miss Harrison asked. "You know Annie had a concussion recently. You might injure her."

Rosie stepped forward, her cheeks red from cold and anger. "Annie did it — she put that mask in my bag, but she won't admit it!"

"I didn't," I cried, "I didn't."

"Why accuse Annie?" Miss Harrison asked.

"Because she was the only one alone in the cloakroom."

Miss Harrison looked at me, long and thoughtfully. "Did you do it, Annie?"

"What if I did? Rosie's mean and bossy, and I hate her!" Elsie was in my head again, speaking in my voice.

Elsie left the swing and floated to the top of a tree. From there, she watched us.

"Come inside, all of you," Miss Harrison said.

Elsie drifted down like a falling leaf and entered the school behind Miss Harrison, imitating her walk.

As Elsie brushed past her, Miss Harrison shivered. "My, it's colder today than I thought," she said. "Much too cold for outside recess, especially for girls who behave like hoydens."

As we took our seats, Miss Harrison summoned me to the front of the room. Elsie came with me, causing Miss Harrison to shiver again and button her jacket.

"Now, Annie, tell us why you put the flu mask in Rosie's bag."

"She made me do it."

"Rosie made you do it?" Miss Harrison asked at the same time Rosie said, "I most certainly did not!"

I wanted to say I didn't mean Rosie, but how could I? Elsie was breathing cold air in my face and freezing the words I wanted to say.

"Tell the class the truth, Annie." Miss Harrison was cross with me. I'd never be one of her favorites again. "Why did you put the mask in Rosie's bag?"

"To scare her, that's all, just to scare her. She always

pretends to be so brave." I glanced at Rosie, feeling her hatred burning right through Elsie's cold presence. "Look at her. She's not as brave as she pretends."

It was as if I couldn't stop talking, even though every word I uttered made Rosie hate me all the more.

"I'm very disappointed in you, Annie," Miss Harrison said. "Yesterday I blamed your behavior on the head injury you suffered, but I'm beginning to think I was mistaken. For some reason, you seem determined to misbehave."

Before she sent me back to my seat, she told me to apologize to Rosie, but Elsie would have none of that. "Rosie deserved it," I heard myself say. "Why should I apologize?"

Shock ran around the classroom like a swarm of wasps. I heard Jane gasp.

Miss Harrison looked as shocked as everyone else. "I want to see you after school, Annie Browne. I'd send you to the cloakroom, but there's no telling what you might do there."

FOURTEEN

WHEN THE DISMISSAL BELL RANG, Rosie, Jane, Eunice, and Lucy lingered in the doorway long enough to give me hateful looks. Thanks to Elsie, who now seemed to control my face, I gave them the same nasty look.

Miss Harrison summoned me to the front of the room. She sat behind her big oak desk, and I stood in front of her. The real me was terrified. I longed to tell her about Elsie, but my new bosom buddy hovered above Miss Harrison and watched me closely. She wouldn't allow me to say anything except what she wanted me to say. I might as well have been her puppet, dancing on strings she controlled and speaking her words with my voice.

"Well, Annie, what do you have to say for yourself?"

"I don't like Rosie. It would serve her right to catch the flu. Elsie caught it. Why shouldn't Rosie?"

"That's a terrible thing to say, Annie."

I leaned across the desk to look her straight in the eye. "You don't know Rosie like *I* know Rosie. You wouldn't believe the mean things she said and did to poor Elsie. She made that girl's life a misery!"

While Elsie laughed, I leaned even closer. "In fact, it might even be Rosie's fault Elsie died."

At this, Elsie turned a somersault in midair.

Miss Harrison looked me in the eye. "What do you mean, Annie?"

"The day before Elsie came down with the flu, Rosie, Lucy, Eunice, and I were in the park. We saw Elsie all by herself swinging in a slow, sad way. She was wearing a flu mask. Rosie said, 'Let's get her,' and she and the others started chasing Elsie and calling her names, but I didn't because I felt sorry for Elsie. She just wanted to be friends with us, that's all, but Rosie said she was a fat ugly Hun and she hated her."

Elsie leaned over Miss Harrison and blew her cold breath on the back of the teacher's neck.

"Something must be wrong with the furnace," Miss Harrison murmured before asking me what happened next.

"They caught up with her, and Rosie grabbed the mask, and they trapped her in a circle and sang the 'in flew Enza' song. It was awful, Miss Harrison. I tried to make them stop, but they got mad and started calling me names too."

I finished Elsie's preferred version of the scene in the park by saying, "If Rosie hadn't chased her, if she hadn't stolen her mask, Elsie would probably be alive today."

Miss Harrison said, "We can't be sure, Annie, but I'm proud of you for sticking up for that unfortunate child."

Elsie was now walking on her hands in circles around Miss Harrison's desk. Her dress had fallen over her head, and I could see her lacy drawers.

I stepped back from the desk. Elsie had begun singing "I see Paris, I see France," and I wanted to get her out of the classroom before she reached the rude part of the song. "Can I go home now, Miss Harrison?"

"Why on earth do you look everywhere but at me?" Miss Harrison asked me. "I don't think you've looked me in the eye once during our entire conversation. It's rude, Annie."

I wanted to tell her I was watching Elsie, but if I did, she'd accuse me of lying. Or of being insane. No matter — Elsie let me say only what she wanted me to say.

I shrugged. "I don't know."

Miss Harrison frowned and tapped her pencil on her desk. "It seems to me I made you stay after school to punish you for something, but I can't remember what it was."

"I can go, then?" Out of the corner of my eye I saw Elsie heading for the cloakroom, and I was worried she might be planning a new prank.

"Yes, yes, go ahead, and please try to behave in class." She smiled a little uncertainly. "You've always been one of my best students."

Followed by my invisible shadow, I left school and walked slowly home.

"It's no fun walking by yourself, is it?" Elsie asked.

I didn't answer, just kept going, head down, hating Elsie more than ever. Poor, unfortunate child, indeed. She'd brought all of this on herself.

And now she was bringing it on me. It wasn't fair. She should be picking on Rosie, not me.

I turned the corner on Portman Street and passed the tall hedge bordering the Steins' house. When I least expected it, Rosie, Lucy, and Eunice leapt out and confronted me.

Rosie pushed her face close to mine so that we were almost nose to nose. "What's wrong with you, have you gone crazy or something?"

"Get away from me!" I shoved Rosie so hard she almost fell down.

"You stink!" Rosie charged at me and pushed me into the hedge. It was the kind that has thorns, and I felt them tear at my clothes and skin.

I struggled to get out of the hedge, but Rosie started punching me, and I fell farther backwards into the thorns. Her fists struck my stomach, my chest, my face. I couldn't get my hands free to defend myself, so I kicked her in the shins.

Rosie staggered back, giving me time to disentangle myself from the hedge. "I hate you," I screamed. "I hate you. You're ugly and common."

A barrage of snowballs hit me, and blood spurted from my nose. I ran for home, and they chased me, just as we'd chased Elsie in the park that day.

I charged into the house and slammed the front door behind me. Safe, I thought, safe from my friends.

But not from Elsie. A closed door couldn't keep her out of the house. "Now you know what it's like to be me!" She danced around, shrieking with laughter.

Mother came running into the hall. "Annie, what happened? Did you fall? Your nose is bleeding, and your face is scratched."

"Rosie pushed me into Mrs. Stein's hedge, the thorny one, and then she and Lucy and Eunice threw snowballs at me and chased me home. They hate me, and I hate them."

While Mother tried to comfort me, Elsie slid down the banister. She'd lost her hair ribbon, and her long, tangled hair hid her face.

"I hate you!" I shouted at her.

Mother gasped. "How dare you speak to me like that!"

With a cry of rage, I broke away from her and ran to the top of the steps. I meant to shove Elsie down the stairs, but my hands went right through her, and I fell instead.

With Elsie's laughter ringing in my ears, I landed at Mother's feet. Her anger gone, she knelt beside me. "Annie, are you all right? Have you broken anything? Did you hit your head?"

I touched my head, afraid it might be bleeding again, but there was no blood and nothing hurt. I sat up cautiously, and Mother helped me to my feet.

"Thank goodness you were still wearing your outdoor clothes," she said. "Your coat and snow pants padded you."

She led me upstairs slowly and carefully, one step at a time, as if I were a toddler just learning to walk.

Elsie watched from the hall chandelier. From the expression on her face, I knew I'd better not try anything like that again. She was already dead. How could she be harmed?

Unlike her, I could definitely be harmed.

In the bathroom, Mother washed my face, wiping the blood away gently so my nose wouldn't begin to bleed again. She dabbed my cuts with iodine, which stung like mad. "Thank goodness you didn't hit your head," she murmured.

After helping me into a warm flannel nightgown, she tucked me into bed. Elsie watched from the shadows, daring me to tell Mother about her.

"I'm worried about you, Annie." Mother sat beside me and stroked my hair. "You haven't been yourself since you hit your head. Are you sure you're well enough to attend school?"

"I don't want to fall behind. Suppose I have to repeat sixth grade?"

"You must promise me not to exert yourself. I'll write Miss Harrison a note to excuse you from gym class and recess until you're fully recovered. Perhaps you should stay indoors at home, as well. This winter has been so cold."

"I'll go to the school library during gym and recess." I smiled at Mother, absolutely delighted. When I had friends instead of enemies, I loved recess, but I'd always hated gym class. Now I dreaded both because they were good opportunities for Rosie and the others to pick on me.

From my rocker in the shadows, Elsie said, "Who's your best friend now? Who's your only friend?"

Just as I was about to yell "Shut up," Mother said, "I'll tell you when dinner's ready, Annie." She kissed me, and I watched her go. Oh, how I yearned to call her back and beg her not to leave me alone with Elsie.

Elsie watched Mother, too. "You don't deserve such a nice mother."

I looked at her in alarm. "What do you mean?"

"Nothing," she said. "Yet."

After dinner, I lingered as long as I could with Mother and Father in the living room. I tried to escape into the dark mystery of *The Moonstone,* but my thoughts kept returning to Elsie. I'd find myself looking around the room, searching shadows and the top of the bookcase for her. I didn't see her, but I knew she was still in the house, probably in my bedroom, plotting and planning her next evil deed.

"Why do you keep staring around the room?" Father asked suddenly.

Keeping my face as blank as possible, I asked, "Am I?"

"Yes, you are. I've been watching you. It's as if you expect to see something that isn't there."

"I guess I was daydreaming."

Mother looked up from the hat she was knitting for me, a blue one with a Nordic pattern and a tassel on top. It was like Rosie's, only hers was green, and I'd wanted it a long time. But not anymore.

"My goodness, Annie, it's eight thirty, way past your bedtime. You've been so quiet I completely forgot you were here."

"It's nice being with you and Father. Can't I stay a little longer?"

"No, indeed. You need your sleep."

"Will you come up with me and tuck me in?"

Father smiled. "A big girl like you?"

"Run along, dear," Mother said. "I'll look in on you later."

Elsie stood in the hall, just outside the band of light from the living room. "I was getting tired of waiting for you."

I followed her upstairs, hating her with a hatred so huge it engulfed my whole self.

FIFTEEN

W HEN I CAME DOWN for breakfast, Elsie floated above me, breathing her cold, moldy breath on my head.

Mother put a steaming bowl of oatmeal on the table. As I began to eat, she said, "I called Rosie's mother last night to complain about her behavior yesterday, but before I spoke a word, ·she told me Rosie has come down with influenza. She's very ill."

I stared at Mother, speechless. "Just like that? She was fine yesterday. She can't be sick —"

From a dark corner by the stove, Elsie snickered. "Thank you, Annie, for doing what I wanted."

Mother regarded me solemnly. "Rosie insists it's your fault she's sick. She told her mother you hid a flu mask with germs on it in her bookbag."

"It was a prank," I said. "That's all. I didn't think it would make her sick." My heart pounded, and I pushed the bowl of oatmeal away. Jumping to my feet, I ran upstairs to the bathroom and vomited into the toilet.

Elsie watched me from the windowsill. "I hope she dies."

"You're a monster," I cried, "and I detest you. Rosie was my friend until you ruined everything. If she dies, I'll think of a way to harm you."

"How can you harm me? I'm already dead."

"Shut up and leave me alone!" I shouted just as Mother entered the bathroom to see if I was all right.

"Annie—" she began, but I pushed past her and ran downstairs. Grabbing my coat, hat, and mittens, I darted outside.

But not fast enough to escape Elsie. Skimming across the snow ahead of me, she called, "Where do you think you're going?"

I stopped on the corner and pulled on my coat, mittens, and hat. I hadn't had time for snow pants and boots, and the icy wind blew through my long stockings. My shoes slipped on the ice.

Ignoring Elsie, I ran toward Rosie's house. It couldn't be true, she couldn't have the flu. Not Rosie.

When I was almost there, I saw Dr. Hughes coming

down the front steps. At the sight of me, he stopped by his car and waited.

"How is she?" I gasped, almost breathless from running.

"Very ill. Her fever's so high she's delirious." He paused and looked at me solemnly. "I'm very concerned about the part you've apparently played in her illness."

I stared at Rosie's bedroom window, its curtains drawn against the light. "I didn't think the mask could hurt her."

"Lucy has told me that your behavior has changed drastically. I know we talked about this earlier when your mother brought you to see me, but it's difficult for me to believe the mild concussion you suffered is responsible."

"You're an ignorant fool." Once again Elsie's words flew out of my mouth. Without looking at him, I turned and ran.

"Annie," he called, "come back here and explain yourself!"

"Run," Elsie said, "run."

I ran behind her. She no longer ran the way she used to, clumsy, arms flapping, but sped like Mercury on winged heels, her dress fluttering, her hair streaming in the wind.

We stopped in front of her house. "Go to my door and knock."

"Why?"

"Just do it."

Helpless to disobey, I climbed the marble steps and lifted the brass knocker. When it thudded against the door, it made a hollow sound, like a stone falling on a coffin lid.

The door slowly opened, and the pale face of Mrs. Schneider peered out at me.

"What do you want?" she asked. "Why aren't you in school?"

Elsie stood beside me, breathing cold air in her stepmother's face. Fearing what she might make me say, I tried to keep my mouth shut, but it opened anyway. "My name is Annie Browne," I said. "I came to tell you that Rosie O'Malley, Jane Anderson, Lucy Hughes, and Eunice Estes are the girls who chased Elsie and stole her flu mask in the park that day. I saw them. They hated her. They were glad she died."

I was about to run away, but Elsie had more to say. "And you were glad, too. You didn't love Elsie. She told me so. And you don't miss her, not even a little bit."

Mrs. Schneider gasped, but without giving her a chance to speak, I dashed down her steps, slipped on the icy sidewalk, picked myself up, and ran.

When the house was out of sight, I stopped and looked

for Elsie. She was sitting on the top of a lamppost, grinning her hideous crooked-toothed grin.

"Why did you make me say those things to your stepmother?" I asked.

Like slowly falling snow, she glided to earth beside me. "She'll tell your mother what you said. Dr. Hughes will probably call your mother too."

She smoothed her hair away from her face. "I just love getting you into trouble. Perfect little Annie Browne isn't so perfect now."

I didn't know what to do or where to go. I was scared to face Mother. I was scared to face Miss Harrison. My friends hated me. I'd made Rosie sick and insulted Dr. Hughes. Without a plan, I walked up one street and down another. My toes were so cold I thought they might snap off.

At last I came to the library. With Elsie tagging along, I climbed the steep stone steps and pushed open the heavy door. Gratefully, I breathed in warm air and its familiar smell of old paper and bookbindings and floor polish. On a weekday morning, it was as quiet as church. A few adults sat at tables in the main reading room, their heads bent over books. The high ceiling echoed with someone's cough, and a man pushed a book cart with squeaky wheels down a row of shelves.

I was hoping to avoid notice, but Miss Jones, one of my favorite librarians, looked up as I passed her desk. "Why, Annie, why aren't you in school?"

"I'm still recovering from a concussion," I told her, relieved to speak my words, not Elsie's.

"Oh, yes, you poor dear. I heard about your sledding mishap on High Street. How do you feel now?"

"Better, but I have headaches and strange dreams," I told her.

"Strange dreams?"

"Yes, Dr. Hughes says dreams and even hallucinations can result from a concussion." Why was I telling Miss Jones this?

I glanced at Elsie. She perched on a book cart by Miss Jones's desk, idly flipping the pages of a dictionary.

"Oh, why can't anyone else see you?" I was startled to hear myself speak my thoughts out loud.

"What do you mean, Annie?" Miss Jones stared at me. "See who?"

"Elsie Schneider. She's right there." I pointed at the book cart. "Are you blind?"

"Elsie's dead," Miss Jones said slowly. "No one is sitting on the cart."

"Can't you see the dictionary pages turning?" My voice

had risen so high it echoed from the ceiling and the marble columns supporting it. People looked up and frowned at me. Someone said, "Hush."

"Annie, come with me." Taking my arm, Miss Jones led me toward her office.

"No, let me go, you stupid cow!" I pulled free and ran out of the library, back into the cold.

"My, my," Elsie said. "The phone's probably ringing at your house already. Your mother is having a lovely morning."

I tried to ignore her, but she skipped ahead and started singing her version of the Enza song.

> Rosie had a little bird,
> And its name was Enza.
> She opened up her window
> And in flew Enza.

She sang it over and over again until I thought I would go mad. I was no longer sure who I was — Annie Browne or Elsie Schneider. I wasn't even sure who'd died, Elsie or me.

Without noticing where I was going, I wandered into the park and sat in a swing, the very swing Elsie had been using the day Rosie had taken her mask.

Elsie sat in the swing next to mine. "This is what friends

do," she said. "They sit together and swing." She pushed off and pointed her bare toes at the cloudy sky. "Come on, Annie, let's see who can go highest."

Without looking at her, I walked away and sat on a bench.

Elsie swung higher and higher. She went right over the top and flew through the air. Landing on a telephone line, she walked back and forth as if she were on a tightrope. "I bet you can't do this," she called.

"Oh, why don't you shut up and leave me alone?"

Just as I spoke, Mother came running across the park, her scarf blowing in the wind. Angrier than I'd ever seen her, she grasped my arm and pulled me up from the bench.

"I've been worried to death about you," she cried. "I didn't know where you'd gone until the phone started ringing, one call after another. First Dr. Hughes, then Mrs. Schneider, and finally Miss Jones. You've been rude and impertinent to all of them, especially poor Mrs. Schneider, who wept into the phone for five minutes before she could tell me what you said to her."

"Ha," Elsie shouted from the telephone line. "Hilda only pretended to be sad. She's glad I'm dead. Glad, glad, glad!" She turned a perfect cartwheel on the telephone line.

"Shut up," I screamed at her. "I hate the sound of your voice!"

Mother began to cry. "Oh, Annie, what's happened to you?"

"Slap her face so hard her nose bleeds," Elsie shrieked at Mother. "Wash her mouth out with laundry soap. Take the hairbrush to her bottom. Lock her in the coal cellar! Do what mothers do!"

Elsie swooped down and seized my hand. Pulling me away from Mother, she ran with me into the park.

Behind us, I heard Mother calling my name. I tried to pull free, but Elsie's hold on me was too strong to break.

SIXTEEN

I DON'T REMEMBER HOW WE GOT THERE, but we ended up at Elsie's grave. She gazed at the tombstones surrounding us. Her eyes moved from her angel to the cross next to it, and then to a series of small, unadorned markers.

"Where would you like to be buried, Annie?"

I stared at her, scared she meant to murder me.

"Perhaps you could be buried right here." She pointed at a patch of snow beside her grave. "We'd be next to each other, bosom friends for all eternity, whispering secrets to each other in the dark. I'd like that — wouldn't you?"

Horrified by the thought, I shook my head. "No," I said. "No, I would not like it."

Elsie stared past me, seemingly not upset by my answer. "When Rosie dies, perhaps her parents will bury *her* here. Perhaps we'll be bosom friends in the grave. Won't you be jealous then?"

"Rosie isn't going to die!" My voice echoed back to me from the mausoleums on the hill.

"If she does, you'll be her murderer. How will you feel then, Annie Browne?"

"She won't die!"

"Will!"

"Won't!"

"Will!"

We were like children on a playground, screaming at each other, our cries bouncing back to us from tombstones.

Elsie suddenly stopped shouting *will* and pointed to a tall oak tree behind me. "Well, well, the crows are back. Nine of them this time." She gave me a sly look. "Do you know what that signifies, Annie?"

I knew, but I was too cold to think of the answer.

"*Eight crows for heaven,*" she recited, "*but nine crows for hell.* And look, here comes one more. *Ten crows for the devil's own self.*"

I hoped it *was* the devil, come to take Elsie away. But the crows flapped their wings and cawed loudly and resettled themselves on the bare branches. They were silhouetted against the pale, bleak sky, and I was reminded of a drawing or maybe an etching I'd seen of crows perched in a tree like that. The picture had a certain grim fascination just as the crows had now.

Elsie returned her attention to me. "Poor Annie, you're *sooo* cold, aren't you? If we stay here much longer, you'll freeze to death."

She settled herself on the angel's shoulder and laughed down at me. "Just think, your frozen body will be found on my grave. Won't that be touching? Like that book, *A Dog of Flanders* — you know, the one where the boy and his dog freeze to death together, in the church."

Shuddering with cold and fear, I wanted to shake Elsie, hit her, hurt her, but I knew she'd drift away from me like smoke and reappear in a different place. "Please," I croaked, "please let me go home."

"First, answer this question, Annie: Which would you prefer? Rosie to die of the flu or you to die of the cold here in the cemetery? Be honest."

"I don't want either Rosie or me to die."

"That's not the answer."

"But it's the truth."

Elsie brushed snow off the angel's wing tips. "No. The truth is you'd choose Rosie to die and you to live. Anyone would. But no one will admit it. Not even to themselves."

Elsie laughed and leapfrogged from tombstone to tombstone, leaving me behind to struggle home through the snow.

I told myself she was wrong. I'd told her the truth. I didn't want either Rosie or me to die. But I couldn't silence the tiny voice that whispered if I really had to choose one of us to die and the other to live, I'd choose Rosie to die and me to live.

All the way home, I prayed, "Please don't let Rosie die, please don't let her die, please don't let her die." Over and over, with every step I took, my prayers rang in my ears. But I never prayed *let me die, not Rosie*. It was always *please don't let Rosie die, please, please, please don't let her die*.

"If you'd prayed like that for me," Elsie whispered from a shadow, "if anyone had, maybe I'd still be alive."

Instead of going home, I walked blocks out of my way to stand in front of Rosie's house. Her window shade was still pulled, but I could see a dim light shining through it.

"Just because her light's on doesn't mean she's alive," Elsie whispered. "No one leaves the dead alone in the dark. Well, not until they're buried."

Ignoring her, I climbed Rosie's steps and rang the bell. I heard footsteps in the hall. The door opened, and Mrs. O'Malley looked down at me.

"What are you doing here, Annie? It's after dark. You should be at home."

"I just wanted to ask how Rosie is."

"She's very ill. I hope you're sorry now about your little prank with the flu mask."

With that, she shut the door.

"Ha," said Elsie. "Mrs. O'Malley blames you. *Everybody* blames you. Think what it will be like when Rosie dies!"

I ran, but I couldn't outrun her. She was always one streetlight ahead, mocking me as she sailed over the snow and ice.

At last I turned the corner and saw my house. The porch light cast sharp shadows across our front yard.

As I ran up the steps, Father opened the door.

"Where have you been this time, Annie?"

"I went to visit my friend Elsie." Of course that was not what I meant to say.

Mother had joined Father in the hall. They stood together and looked at me, their faces drawn with worry.

"You walked all the way to the cemetery?" Father asked.

"You didn't even like that girl," Mother added.

"Elsie was my bosom friend, but I kept it secret because of the others."

Mother stared at me. "What others?"

"Rosie, Jane, Lucy, Eunice." I spat their names out as if they were poison.

"I thought they were your friends," Father said.

"You don't know what they're really like. I kept my friendship with Elsie secret from them because they hated her. It was Rosie's fault Elsie died of flu. She stole her flu mask."

"I don't understand," Mother said.

"You don't understand." I was mocking Mother now. I wanted to stop and beg her forgiveness, but Elsie wouldn't let me. "What do you know about me or who my friends are or what I do or what I think? Nothing!"

Elsie's words continued to pour from my mouth. She was in my head. She'd taken possession of me; she could make me say anything she wanted me to say. Lie after lie.

"You don't care about me! You pretend to love me, oh yes, but secretly you wish I'd die of the flu like poor Elsie!"

As I broke away and ran to my room, I heard Mother ask Father, "Now do you believe me? She's been acting like this ever since she returned to school."

He said, "Perhaps we need to find a different doctor."

I slammed my bedroom door and flung myself on my bed. Elsie sat beside me.

"A different doctor. Hmm." She ran her icy fingers

through my hair. "I'm afraid you might end up in the state lunatic asylum out on the Baltimore Pike. Padded cells, straitjackets, cold baths, but don't worry, I'll come to visit you. You'll always have me, no matter what."

"I hate you so much I'd kill you all over again if I could!"

It was at that moment Mother opened my door. "What did you just say, Annie? Who would you kill?"

"Nobody! Leave me alone. I don't want you near me."

Mother hesitated in the doorway.

I was throwing my pillows at her and screaming words I didn't know I knew.

Mother backed away and called Father.

By the time he ran up the steps, I was hurling my collection of china figurines at the wall. My precious little dogs and cats, horses and squirrels, birds and rabbits, broke into fragments. Heads, legs, wings, and tails lay scattered on the floor. My elephant, a gift from Great-aunt Violet and the largest and heaviest thing on the shelf, crashed through my window and disappeared into the night, followed by Edward Bear.

Before Father restrained me, I'd thrown my books at him and Mother, yanked the head off Antoinette, and kicked over the dollhouse.

Panting and struggling to escape his arms, I continued

to swear. Mother was crying, but Elsie was perched on my bureau clapping her hands with delight.

"For God's sake, Ida," Father shouted, "call Dr. Hughes!"

By the time, the doctor arrived, I'd fallen asleep from exhaustion. I woke to see him bending over me.

"Go away!" My voice was so hoarse from shouting it was no more than a raspy whisper.

"What's troubling you, Annie?" he asked.

"Nothing. Everything. The moon, the sun, the stars."

He looked puzzled. "Is that all?"

I think he meant to try a little humor, but it didn't work.

"The world," I whispered, "and all the people in it. Especially you." I grabbed his arm. "Just make her go away. Then I'll be me."

"Who?"

Elsie sat in my rocking chair, smiling to herself. To my surprise, she let me go on in my own words.

"Elsie Schneider, that's who." I pointed at the rocking chair. "Can't you see her sitting there?"

Dr. Hughes looked at the chair. "Annie," he said softly, "Elsie passed away last fall. She isn't here."

I grabbed his arm. I had to make him believe me. "Oh, yes she is, only no one sees her or hears her but me. She's gotten inside me. She makes me say things, she makes me do things, like putting the flu mask in Rosie's bookbag. She wanted Rosie to get the flu, she wants her to die and be buried next to her."

"Why are you telling me this?"

"Because somebody has to make her go away."

"Listen to me, Annie. You're fatigued—you need to rest. I'm going to give you a pill to help you relax and sleep."

He handed me a glass of water and big white pill. I swallowed it and drank all of the water to wash away the bitter taste it left in my mouth.

He sat beside me until the pill took effect. The last thing I saw was Elsie. She was perched on Dr. Hughes's shoulder, grinning down at me. Then everything whirled away into darkness.

SEVENTEEN

WHEN I AWOKE, I thought I was still dreaming. The room in which I found myself was pleasant enough, but it wasn't my room. How had I gotten there?

In a state of panic, I sat up and called Mother and Father. Where were they? Where was I?

"I know where you are." Elsie sat down on the bed and leaned toward me. She looked very pleased with herself. "Admit it — you know, too."

I shook my head. I was still groggy from the pill Dr. Hughes had given me, and there was a bitter taste in my mouth. My thoughts were crooked, random. They rolled through my head without connecting with one another.

"Am I sick? Am I in the hospital?"

Elsie laughed. "Maybe, maybe not," she said. "Go on, guess again."

I looked around, frantic to find a clue, but the pale blue walls told me nothing.

Elsie sighed. "You could call it a hospital. Some people do. And they definitely think you're sick." She spun her finger and tapped her forehead.

"What are you talking about? I'm not crazy — why would I be in an insane asylum?"

"Have you forgotten the trouble you got into yesterday?"

"But that was your fault. You made me do those things!"

At that moment, the door opened and a doctor I'd never seen came in. Mother and Father followed him. Mother tried to run to my side, but Father stopped her. "Remember, Annie mustn't be overexcited," he whispered as if I weren't meant to hear. "She needs a calm atmosphere and plenty of rest."

"What did you just say?" the doctor asked me.

"I wasn't talking to you."

"Who were you talking to?"

"Nobody." I lay down and pulled the cover up to my chin.

Elsie flitted about the room singing, *"I ain't got no body, and nobody cares for me."* The curtains stirred as she passed the window, the armchair moved a smidgen closer to my bed, a picture on the wall tipped to the right, but no one noticed any of this. Their attention was fixed on me, the crazy girl.

"Why am I in an insane asylum?" I shouted to be heard over Elsie's racket. "I'm not sick, I'm not crazy, I want to go home!"

"I'm Dr. Benson," the man said in a soft voice, probably meant to calm me. "You're in the Cedar Grove Convalescent Home, not an insane asylum. You're neither sick nor crazy, but your concussion has left you in a precarious state of mind. You're here to get the rest and treatment you need. Depending on your progress and cooperation, you'll be with us a month or so."

"I hope you're satisfied!" I shouted at Elsie, who was now standing next to Father, smirking at me.

Father stared at me. "Why should I be satisfied, Annie? Believe me, this is the last thing I want for you, but after last night—"

It was rude, I know, but I interrupted him. "I wasn't talking to you, Father."

Dr. Benson looked around the room with exaggerated

care and said, "I don't see anyone here but your father, your mother, and me."

"That's the whole problem," I cried. "No one sees her but me."

"We're concerned about your insistence that Elsie Schneider is here," the doctor said, still speaking in that soft, low voice. "Surely you know she died last fall."

He paused and looked at me closely. "Do you feel guilty about Elsie's death? Did you say or do something you regret?"

"Yes, you did, yes, indeed you did," Elsie hissed, "and I'm here to make you pay for it."

"It wasn't just me — it was all of us — but she's taking it out on me. She won't leave me alone. She says she's my bosom buddy, but I HATE HER!" I was screaming and crying and trying to say everything before Elsie stopped me and filled my mouth with her words.

"And now she's here in this very room," I babbled on. "She torments me day and night and makes me say and do terrible things!"

When I finally ran out of words, I looked at Elsie. She smiled as if my performance pleased her.

Dr. Benson spoke to my parents in a whisper. I couldn't hear his remarks, but whatever he said made Elsie smile wide enough to show her nasty teeth, stained as if she'd been eating dirt.

A servant arrived with my breakfast, a soft-boiled egg in a cup, toast soldiers, and orange juice — just what I had at home.

While I picked at the food, Dr. Benson told my parents they could stay with me for a couple of hours.

"After you leave," he went on, "Annie will eat lunch and begin a program of activities designed especially for her. Arts and crafts, calisthenics, a tutor to help with her school work. If all goes well, she'll be permitted to spend an unsupervised hour or so in the library. Of course, she'll see me at least once every day."

"You'll like that, won't you?" Mother asked me. "You've always enjoyed arts and crafts, and it will be good to keep up with your schoolwork."

In hope I'd be free of Elsie during the activities designed just for me, the girl in a precarious state of mind, I nodded enthusiastically. Everyone looked pleased — except Elsie. I knew she detested being left out.

Dr. Benson excused himself. As he left the room, Elsie made faces at him, but of course no one but me noticed.

Father took a seat in an armchair near my bed, Mother sat on the bed beside me, and Elsie swung by her knees from the curtain rod, hair hanging over her face, showing off her lacy bloomers again.

After I'd eaten what I could, Mother carried the tray to a small table near the door. Returning to her seat beside me, she touched my hand gently. "You know Elsie isn't here, Annie."

"And she's not responsible for your behavior," Father added.

"She's right there." I pointed at Elsie. "Why can't you see her?"

"Nobody's there, Annie." Mother was close to tears, but Elsie crowed with laughter.

"She's right," Elsie said. *"I ain't got no body!"*

"Shut up!" I yelled at her.

Mother drew away from me, but Father said, "Remember, Ida, Annie's not talking to you. She's talking to Elsie."

When Mother gave in to tears, Father left his chair and sat beside me on the bed. Putting an arm around me, he said, "You must believe me. Elsie is a figment of your imagination. That's why no one else can see her."

"Oh, Father." I pressed my face against his jacket and wept. He and Mother did their best to comfort me, but it was hopeless. As long as they believed Elsie to be a figment of my imagination, they couldn't help me. No one could.

For the rest of their visit, Mother and Father tried to cheer me up. We played a couple of games of Parcheesi, and I won both. Probably they let me win — anything to keep the crazy girl happy. Father said it was because my friends and I played Parcheesi often and he and Mother hadn't played for years. They were out of practice.

Next Father pulled a set of Author cards out of his jacket pocket. I was the first to match my four authors with their books — Charles Dickens, Sir Walter Scott, Nathaniel Hawthorne, and Louisa May Alcott. Father almost won, but I managed to edge him out with *Oliver Twist,* thereby completing my last set.

Mother was hopelessly behind, which made her laugh. "I need to read something besides cookbooks."

"It's a matter of getting the right cards," Father said. "Winning has nothing to do with reading the author's books."

We began another round. As we asked each other for cards, I think we all forgot where I was and why. But I couldn't help wondering what Elsie was doing while we amused ourselves with games. She was very quiet — no interruptions, no taunts, no antics. From time to time, not often enough for my parents to notice, I looked around the room. Morning sunlight cast shadows as it streamed through the windows, but Elsie wasn't hiding in them. Nor was she behind Father's chair, lurking in corners, or hanging upside down from the curtain rod. She was definitely not here, and I began to hope she really was a figment of my imagination.

Just as we finished our third game of Authors, which Mother won, a nurse entered the room and told Father and Mother that visiting hours were over for the day. Mother hugged me tearfully and begged me to get well and come home soon. Father presented me with a couple of books he and Mother had picked out — *Seventeen* and *Anne's House of Dreams*.

"I hope you haven't read these yet," he said as he put them on the bedside table.

"Oh, I've been especially wanting to read *Seventeen*. I've heard it's very funny, much like the Penrod books, which you know I love. Only for someone a little older — like me."

I picked up *Anne's House of Dreams*. "This is the newest. I've read all the ones that came before."

I didn't tell Father I'd lost interest in the Anne books now that Elsie had entered my life. It hurt to read them and think of Rosie and the fun we had when we were friends.

I hugged them both. "Please come tomorrow."

After they left my room, I listened to their footsteps until I couldn't hear them anymore. They hadn't wanted to go — I knew that — but I slid under the covers and cried until a woman entered the room. She introduced herself as Nurse Baker. From the way she looked at me, I was certain she knew all about me and my precarious state of mind.

"It's almost time for lunch, Annie," she said in a no-nonsense manner. "Time to get out of bed, wash, and dress. You must look presentable when you meet the others."

"The others?"

"You'll take your meals in the dining room, just like everyone else. No pampering for you, my girl."

I disliked Nurse Baker already. She was cross and sharp-spoken and bossy. I almost wished Elsie were here to torment her in some way.

Without looking at her, I washed my face and hands in the bowl she'd brought. I used the pot she pulled out from under the bed, although it mortified me to do so. I put on the plain blue dress she gave me, thick stockings, and un-fashionable button-top shoes.

"Why can't I wear my own clothes?"

"We don't want anyone having nicer things than some-one else." With that, she handed me a brush and comb and a hair ribbon.

When I was washed, dressed, and combed, she looked me over and frowned. "I suppose you'll do."

I followed Nurse Baker down a long straight hall lined

with open doors. Each room was exactly like mine. I hadn't thought to look at the number and hoped I could find it when lunch was over.

Before we entered the dining room, she gave me a schedule of my activities. "Don't forget," she said, "arts and crafts in Room 30-B immediately after lunch. Be on time. Punctuality is important."

With that, she handed me over to a tall, dour woman wearing a black dress with a white apron over it and a small white cap on her head. Without a smile, she told me to follow her.

Despite the number of people sitting at several long tables, the dining room was quiet. Everyone looked at me as I walked past, but no one smiled or said hello.

They were all much older than I was, most of them adults at least Mother's age, but some quite elderly. They didn't smile, just looked. Was smiling forbidden?

I felt lost and sad. It was Elsie who belonged here, not me, but whoever heard of putting a ghost into a convalescent home?

The woman seated me at the end of a table. My chair faced the window. Outside the winter sun sparkled on snow, and I wished I were free to leave the dining room and go outside.

The women at the table glanced at me and continued

chatting about their various ailments and unappreciative relatives. I supposed they thought someone as young as I was could be of no interest to them. Certainly I had nothing to contribute to their conversational topics. Except for Elsie — describing her might stop the talking entirely. And convince them that I was truly a lunatic.

The old lady sitting beside me caught my eye and smiled. She had a kind face, but her eyes were sad. "My name is Mrs. Jameson," she said in a voice so low I had to lean close to hear her.

"I'm Annie Browne."

"Annie — I've never met a person named Annie I didn't like." She smiled again. "Don't let those women hurt your feelings," she told me. "They're decidedly unfriendly. I've been here a week and haven't exchanged one word with them. Not even hello."

She paused a moment, but before I said anything, she added, "Perhaps you and I can become friends."

I wasn't sure a girl my age could be friends with a woman her age, but I needed someone to talk to. I'd pretend she was my grandmother. With her pink cheeks and white hair, she certainly looked the part.

"That would be nice," I told her.

"Do you enjoy reading?" she asked.

"Oh, yes, I love to read." While we ate our chicken noodle soup, we talked about books. We both enjoyed Wilkie Collins and Charles Dickens. She recommended Willa Cather's novels, and I recommended *Seventeen*. She told me she'd loved *The Magnificent Ambersons,* Tarkington's best book, she claimed. "But perhaps a bit slow, compared to Penrod's antics."

When the meal ended, the other women walked away, still engrossed in conversation, but Mrs. Jameson lingered a moment. Taking my hand, she said, "I've enjoyed talking to you, Annie Browne." She paused and peered into my eyes before adding, "I hope you don't mind my saying so, but something about you worries me."

"Oh, you needn't be concerned about me," I said quickly. "I'm not crazy or anything like that. I crashed my sled and got a concussion. Dr. Benson says it's left me in a precarious state of mind. That's why I'm here." I smiled and shrugged to emphasize I was fine, no cause for her to worry.

Mrs. Jameson held my hand tighter, as if she feared I might run from her. "No," she said softly. "It's more than that. You're frightened. I see it in your eyes."

I looked away, but I didn't pull my hand from hers. I longed to tell her what really frightened me, but she'd never believe it. So, keeping Elsie a secret, I said, "I'm scared Dr.

Benson will make me stay in Cedar Grove for a long, long time. I want to go home. I miss Mother and Father. I miss my friends and school and sleeping in my own bed at night."

"Of course you do. I miss my family and my home, too." Mrs. Jameson looked at me closely. "But something else is weighing heavily upon you, Annie. I don't know what it is, but I sense deep sorrow, loneliness, fear —"

Before I had a chance to speak, a crew of cleaning women entered the room. Some carried mops and buckets; others carried trays and rags. One of them scowled at Mrs. Jameson. "Lunch is over," she said. "The dining room is closed until dinner. We need to clean up, you know."

"I beg your pardon," Mrs. Jameson said. "We'll leave at once."

Still holding my hand, she led me into the hall. "We don't have time to talk now," she said, "but if you ever wish to confide in me, I'll be happy to listen. And to help you if I can."

Giving me a pat on the shoulder, Mrs. Jameson walked away. I watched her go. In the sunlight streaming through the windows, her white hair shone.

After she turned a corner, I lingered in the hall. What did Mrs. Jameson sense about me? What worried her? What did she see in my eyes?

"You," someone called to me, "what are you doing in

the hall?" A stern-faced woman in a black skirt and white blouse approached me.

"I'm supposed to be in arts and crafts," I told her, "but I can't find the room."

"Come with me," she said. "And hurry. You're already late."

Silently I followed her down the hall, relieved that I hadn't gotten into trouble.

EIGHTEEN

ARTS AND CRAFTS met in a big sunny room with tall windows on one wall. Patients sat on stools at high tables. Everyone was making clay bowls.

A plump, rosy-faced woman approached me. "I'm Miss Ellis," she said, "and you must be Annie Browne."

I looked at her smiling face and wondered what she knew about me. "I'm sorry I'm late," I apologized. "I couldn't find the room."

"It's a big place, but you'll figure it out in no time." She led me to a table under a window and introduced me to the three women already sitting there. They glanced at me and returned to their conversation. As usual, they made no effort to include me. I was a child, of no interest to them.

Miss Ellis gave me a ball of gray clay. "We're making pots today. Be creative," she said in a perky voice. "Express yourself, Annie."

I studied the damp clay with distaste. It was cold and slippery, and I hated the way it felt. I looked at Miss Ellis in hope she'd give me a hint about making a pot, but she'd gone to the other side of the room to help an old lady. Not knowing what else to do, I rolled out snakelike coils of clay and fashioned a lopsided bowl. It looked as if a kindergartner had made it.

Clumsy as it was, Miss Ellis raved as if it were a masterpiece. Surely she saw my bowl for what it was—a misshapen mud ball. When she wasn't looking, I mashed the bowl with my fist, rolled the clay into a ball, and stuck it to the underside of the table.

Next, I spent an hour with Dr. Benson. We'd barely gotten through the niceties of *how are you, I'm fine,* when he asked if Elsie had joined us.

I said quite honestly she wasn't there.

He leaned toward me, obviously pleased with my response. While he asked more questions, mainly about Elsie, her death, and my feelings about it, my mind raced ahead. Even if Elsie returned, I'd tell Dr. Benson and my parents she was gone. I'd say perhaps she'd been a figment of my

imagination after all. I'd say I felt terrible about teasing Elsie the day before she caught flu. I'd say I was sorry I hadn't
at least tried to defend her. I'd say she wasn't really as bad as
everyone thought. I'd say she hadn't deserved to be treated
so badly.

Mostly lies, but I was certain it was what Dr. Benson
and Elsie wanted to hear. If I kept Elsie's presence to myself,
maybe he'd let me go home.

When Dr. Benson told me my hour was over, he said,
"I'm very pleased with the progress we've made today. If
you continue to do well, Annie, perhaps you can go home in
a week or so."

I almost skipped for joy on the way to my room. Dr.
Benson was pleased. We were making progress. If my state
of mind was less precarious, he might send me home as
soon as next week. I'd be good, so good. I wouldn't get into
trouble. No matter what she did, I'd resist Elsie. If I ignored
her, maybe she'd give up and go back to the cemetery. How
happy I'd be then.

All those thoughts came to a stop when I opened the
door to my room. Elsie grinned at me from her perch on
the curtain rod. She'd found a red crayon somewhere and
scrawled bad words on the walls. She'd drawn naughty pictures as well, crudely done but recognizable as certain body
parts no one ever mentions.

In despair, I looked at what she'd done. How was I to explain it? Who could have done it but me?

"What a bad girl you've been, Annie," Elsie said with that hideous smirk of hers. "I had no idea you knew so many naughty words. And those pictures. What will Dr. Benson say when he sees this?"

Elsie dropped to the floor and skipped across the room to me. "Instead of sending you home," she said, "he'll pack you off to the lunatic asylum. But don't worry, I'll go with you. I'll never desert you, never, never, never."

With that, she jumped out the window and left me to deal with what she'd done. Shaking with rage, I tried to wipe the words and drawings off the walls, but I succeeded only in smearing my hands with red crayon.

Behind me, the door opened, and I heard a gasp. I whirled around to see Nurse Baker staring at the wall, clearly horrified by Elsie's handiwork.

"Good Lord," she cried. "What kind of a girl are you?"

"I didn't do this!"

"Don't lie to me! Just look at your hands—you've got red crayon all over them."

"I was trying to clean it off." My voice rose. "I don't even know what the words mean!"

"I'm sending for Dr. Benson!"

"No, no, please don't tell him. Please, I beg you." I

threw myself at her and tried to keep her from leaving. "You must believe me, I didn't do this, I didn't!"

She freed herself from me. "You're hysterical!" Without warning, Nurse Baker drew her arm back and slapped my face so hard I almost fell down.

"What's going on here?" Dr. Benson stood in the doorway. "I heard the noise from my office."

"I didn't do it," I wailed. "Elsie did. She's not gone, after all."

"I caught Annie Browne in the act," Nurse Baker told him. "Just look at her hands."

"I'm looking at the red mark on her face. Did you slap her?"

"The girl was hysterical. In my family, a good slap always put an end to that sort of behavior."

"We do not strike patients here, Nurse Baker. One more incident like this, and you will be dismissed without a recommendation. Please leave now. I'll deal with Annie."

Nurse Baker sniffed and left the room in a huff. As soon as she was gone, Dr. Benson turned his attention to the wall. "What's the meaning of this, Annie? I thought you were making real progress, but now . . ." He frowned. "Are you blaming Elsie?"

"Yes," I cried. "Yes. Who else could have done it?"

He gazed at me sadly. "Who else, indeed?"

Even though he didn't believe me, I said it again. "*Elsie* did it. She hates me. Don't you see? She wants to make me pay for not being her friend."

"When will you give up this obsession with Elsie? The girl died months ago. She can't make you do anything. Whether you admit or not, you defaced this wall. *You*, Annie, no one but you."

No, I thought, *I didn't, I didn't, I didn't*. It made no sense to say it out loud. The more I insisted Elsie was real, the crazier I seemed.

Dr. Benson went to the door and looked back at me. "I'll have someone bring you a bucket of soapy water and rags so you can scrub off this filth."

I sat on my bed and stared at Elsie's handiwork. There was no chance now of going home next week. Or even next month.

What was to become of me? Only a crazy girl would insist a ghost was responsible for those words and drawings. Only a crazy girl would blame a dead girl. I was sure I wasn't crazy. I was sure Elsie was real . . . but what if she wasn't? What if I really was crazy?

My thoughts were interrupted by a cleaning woman. Setting down a bucket of soapy water and a handful of rags, she stared at the wall.

"Shocking," she said. "Shocking that a young girl like yourself should know such things."

Looking at me as if I were a demon, she left the room and shut the door behind her.

With a sigh, I dipped the rag into the water and began to scrub. And scrub and scrub. I scrubbed until my arms ached, but the words and drawings remained, paler, harder to see, but still visible.

Part of my punishment was to eat dinner in my room. That was fine with me. Except for Mrs. Jameson, I didn't enjoy the company of the others.

Nurse Baker brought my tray. She looked at the wall and sniffed in disgust. "I can still see those words and drawings. Your room will need a few coats of paint to cover them up. That will cost your father a pretty penny."

"I did my best," I muttered, "but —"

"Your best wasn't good enough, was it?" Nurse Baker put my dinner tray down and left the room. Her starched skirts rustled in disapproval. She probably thought a few more slaps might improve me.

After I finally fell asleep, Elsie woke me by snatching off my covers. She'd brought the cold of winter with her, and I tried to pull my blanket back. Taking the blanket with her, she leapt to the top of my wardrobe and grinned at me.

"I see they made you scrub the wall," she said. "Didn't they like my artwork?"

I huddled on my bed, shivering without my covers. "I hate you."

Elsie laughed. "Didn't you miss me? Didn't you wonder where I went?"

"Wherever it was, I wish you'd stayed there."

"If you insist, I'll tell you. Or even if you don't insist, I'll tell you anyway." She jumped down from the wardrobe, leaving the blanket out of my reach. "I went to Rosie's house, to see how she is, poor girl."

She paused. "Aren't you going to ask me how your former best friend is?"

I hugged my knees tight to my chest and waited. The gleeful expression on her face scared me.

"Well, I'm happy to tell you my plan worked. Rosie died last night."

"No," I whispered. "That can't be true. You're lying. You always lie."

"Except when I tell the truth," Elsie said. "Which happens to be what I'm doing now. I saw Rosie in her coffin, laid out in the parlor just like I was. As dead as dead can be."

"No, no, no," I whispered.

"Yes, yes, yes!" Elsie hopped around the room singing, "I had a little bird, and I named her Enza. I opened Rosie's window, and in flew Enza!"

I pulled the pillow over my head, but I could still hear her.

Snatching the pillow away, she leaned over me. "And guess what else? Everybody says it's *your* fault. You put that mask in her bookbag and she caught flu and now she's dead. You murdered her, everyone says so, and you'll go to jail for the rest of your miserable life!"

"You made me put the mask in Rosie's bag!" I screamed.

"And how will you prove that?"

"I hate you! You're a monster," I screamed.

Elsie laughed again and returned to the top of my wardrobe. "What a nice warm blanket," she called. "Thanks for giving it to me."

Nearly frozen, I huddled on my bed and wept. I saw Rosie laughing, skipping rope, bouncing a ball, and shouting, "One, two, three O'Leario." Rosie my friend, Rosie the wild girl, more fun than anyone in the world. I saw her sick with flu, drenched with perspiration, burning with fever, hallucinating. I saw her still and cold and white, lying in her coffin while Jane and Lucy and Eunice wept. And blamed me.

Why had I put the mask in Rosie's bookbag? Why hadn't I fought Elsie? What kind of a person was I?

And all the while, as I lay there tormenting myself with guilt, Elsie perched above me on the headboard of my bed, swinging her bare feet in my face and singing, "The worms crawl in, the worms crawl out, the worms play pinochle on your snout. They eat your eyes, they eat your nose, they eat the jelly between your toes."

NINETEEN

ON THE MORNING, Elsie was gone, and my blanket was on the floor. Wrapping it around me, I sat on my bed and wept again for Rosie.

A nurse came to remind me I was expected to be in the dining room for breakfast. She was new. Maybe Nurse Baker had quit and I'd never see her again. I told the nurse I wasn't hungry.

She looked at me closely. "Have you been crying?"

I wiped my nose with the back of my hand. "Yes."

"I guess you're sorry about what you did to your room." She looked at the wall and shook her head. "I see you didn't scrub it all off."

"I tried." I sniffled and snuffled.

"I'll bring breakfast to your room. I'm sure Dr. Benson

will want to see you as soon as you've finished eating." She turned to leave but stopped to say, "In the meantime, get dressed, Annie. Comb your hair. Wash your face."

I did as she asked, but I didn't eat the breakfast she brought. Nor did I go to see Dr. Benson. I'd caused Rosie's death. How was I to face anyone?

A little later, Dr. Benson found me sitting in my rocking chair, looking out the window.

"Nurse O'Brien told me you've been crying," Dr. Benson said. His voice was gentler than usual. "I suppose you're upset about last night. Nurse Baker shouldn't have slapped you."

I shook my head. "I just found out my friend Rosie has died of the flu and—" I broke down again.

"Oh, I'm so sorry, Annie. That's sad news indeed." He sat down on my bed and looked at me with sympathy. "But who told you? How do you know?"

Before I could stop myself, I blurted, "Elsie told me last night. She says it's my fault. She says I murdered Rosie, and I'll be sent to jail, but it's *her* fault, not mine! She made me kill Rosie."

Dr. Benson's expression changed from sympathetic to disappointed. "Oh, Annie, I've told you again and again, Elsie is dead. She can't tell you anything. She exists in your mind and nowhere else."

"If you'd just try, you'd see her yourself. She's outside right now." I pointed at Elsie, who was pirouetting on the lawn. "Why can't you admit she's there? You must see her, you must!"

"Please, Annie, stop shouting. Take a deep breath, relax." Dr. Benson took my hand. "Now, tell me why you think you killed Rosie."

Even though I knew it was useless to explain, I said, "Elsie hated Rosie. She wanted her to die. She made me put her flu mask in Rosie's bookbag, and Rosie caught the flu, and now she's dead."

"Oh, Annie, my dear child, where do you get these ideas? You didn't kill your friend. The flu did."

"But the mask," I cried. "It was full of Elsie's germs."

"The mask had nothing to do with it." He shook his head. "And neither did Elsie. It's very unfortunate that your friend died, but no one, least of all you, is responsible for her death."

I looked outside. Elsie had climbed into a tree near the window and made herself comfortable on a branch. She swung her feet and made faces at me. Laughing, she flipped over to hang by her knees from the branch. If the window had been open, I could have touched her.

"Give up, Annie," she said. "He's never going to believe

you, and neither is anyone else. The more you say, the cra-zier people think you are. Didn't I tell you I was a secret not to reveal? Yet you blab and blab and blab and blame me for everything."

While Elsie jeered at me, Dr. Benson rang for a nurse and asked her to bring warm milk and buttered toast for me.

"I don't want milk or toast."

"You didn't eat your breakfast."

"I'm not hungry."

"You need nourishment."

When Nurse O'Brien came back with a tray, I found I was hungry after all. I'd no sooner drunk the milk and eaten the toast than I realized I was very tired. I lay on my bed and closed my eyes.

Dr. Benson covered me with a blanket. "A good nap is just what you need, Annie." His voice sounded far away. I was asleep before he left the room.

The next thing I knew, Nurse Baker was shaking me awake. "It's almost lunchtime, you lazy girl."

Still groggy from my nap, I stared at her in confusion.

"Did you hear me?" she asked. "Get ready for lunch. Now."

"I don't feel well," I told her.

"Do as you're told." She scowled at me, her face creased

with dislike. "I have no time to spare for a girl like you."
With that, she left the room. The door slammed shut behind her.

I stood up slowly. Even though I'd been asleep, I was tired. And lightheaded. Too dazed to stand, I sank down on the bed and stared about me in confusion.

How long had I been asleep? And why was I so sad?

"You know why you're sad." Elsie materialized from the shadows behind the wardrobe. "Here's a hint — somebody died. I hated her. You liked her. So I'm glad and you're sad."

It came back to me then — Rosie was dead, and it was my fault. I'd be sent to jail. Or to the state lunatic asylum.

"Go away," I screamed at Elsie. "Go away and leave me alone!"

The door opened, and Dr. Benson stood on the threshold. "What is it now, Annie? Why are you screaming at me?"

I shook my head and said nothing. What was the sense of telling him I was screaming at Elsie? She was gone now anyway. The cold air she'd left behind eddied around my ankles and chilled me all the way to my knees.

Dr. Benson smiled at me. "Now that you're finished screaming at me, you might like to hear some good news."

For a moment, I hoped he'd say he was sending me home, but instead he said, "I phoned your mother while you were sleeping and asked her about Rosie." He took my hands in his. "Rosie isn't dead, Annie. In fact, she's out of danger now. Your mother has no idea where you got that notion. She told me Dr. Hughes expects Rosie to be back in school in a few weeks."

I stared at him, afraid to believe what he was saying. "But Elsie said —"

He pressed a finger to his lips. "Not another word about Elsie. You must have dreamed Elsie told you Rosie was dead. Believe me, Rosie is alive and recovering. Concentrate on her, and forget about Elsie. She doesn't exist."

Oh, if only that were true. At this very moment, Elsie was perched on top of the wardrobe, making faces at Dr. Benson. While I watched, she took a pebble out of her pocket and threw it at him.

The pebble struck his leg and startled him. Puzzled, he looked around. When nothing else happened, he shrugged and laughed. "Now you've got me imagining things, Annie."

Without noticing the pebble on the floor, he suggested going to lunch. We walked to the dining room with Elsie behind us, and Dr. Benson shivered. "The hall's drafty today," he said. "I'll have someone check the furnace."

At the dining room door, Dr. Benson told me to eat a good lunch. "Cheer up," he said. "Smile. We'll talk soon."

Elsie followed me into the room and whispered in my ear. "He's an idiot. *Cheer up, smile, we'll talk soon* — what nonsense."

In the cold air Elsie stirred up, people buttoned their sweaters and complained about the chill.

Without looking at anyone, I made my way to my seat across from the window and stared at the snowy lawn. Someone had made a row of snowmen along the driveway, and in the blink of an eye, Elsie had gone outside to knock their heads off one by one. I watched her snatch a tall silk hat from a snowman and put it on her head. Then she took a long red scarf from another and wrapped it around her neck.

Mrs. Jameson tapped my shoulder. "My goodness, Annie, look outside. The wind must be very strong. The snowmen are losing their heads. See?"

She pointed as Elsie toppled the last one. "Isn't that strange?" she asked.

It was indeed strange. Stranger than Mrs. Jameson realized.

"It's almost as if somebody is knocking off their heads," she said slowly. "You don't see anyone out there, do you?"

I almost choked on my soup. "No, no, of course not. Do you see anyone?"

"For a moment, I could have sworn I saw —" She shook her head. "No, I'm mistaken. How silly of me. It's just a hat blowing in the wind. And a scarf."

But Mrs. Jameson continued to gaze out the window as if she saw Elsie running across the snow, the long red scarf streaming behind her.

Mrs. Coakley leaned across the table to get Mrs. Jameson's attention. "I don't know why you waste your time talking to that girl. Have you heard what she did to the walls of her room? She scribbled dirty words and dirty pictures all over them. She's a guttersnipe with a filthy mind."

Mrs. Jameson stared at her. "I don't believe you, Hester. Annie is a sweet child. She'd never do something that vile."

Mrs. Coakley shrugged. "If you don't believe me, ask someone else. It's been the talk of Cedar Grove." She leaned closer. "Here's the amazing part: she swears she didn't do it. I ask you — who else could have done it?"

"I'm not a liar!" I shouted. "I didn't do it!"

A murmur ran around the room. I'd spoken louder than I'd meant to.

Mrs. Coakley drew herself up like a balloon about to explode. "How dare you speak to me like that! I've a good mind to report you."

One of the servers looked our way, and Mrs. Jameson

took my arm. "Come with me, Annie. Mrs. Coakley needs a moment to calm down."

The two of us left the room. No one said anything, but I could sense their disapproval as they watched us go by. As soon as we were in the hall, I heard the buzz of whispered conversations. *Shocking, disgusting, what sort of home does she come from . . .*

"Let's go someplace where we can talk," Mrs. Jameson suggested. "We have half an hour of free time."

We found a seat in a quiet corner in the library, but I couldn't relax until I'd studied every shadow and every dark corner for signs of Elsie. She came and went so quickly — she could be anywhere. If she saw me talking to Mrs. Jameson, she'd do something horrible, I knew she would.

"What's worrying you, Annie?" Mrs. Jameson asked. "You're a bundle of nerves today."

"Nothing, I'm fine." I fidgeted with my hair. Had I remembered to comb it?

"Did Mrs. Coakley upset you?"

"I didn't scribble those things on my wall."

"Perhaps you've just forgotten," she said. "Sometimes I do things I don't remember. I'm told I broke all my wedding china the day my husband died. Threw it against the wall and smashed every single plate, cup, and saucer. I suppose

I was out of my mind with grief. Perhaps it was something like that with you. You were upset, angry, sad—"

"No, it's not like that. I *know* I didn't do it. Someone else did." I should have stopped talking then, but the words came tumbling out and I couldn't control them. "She says she's my friend, but she's not. She hates me, and she won't leave me alone. She goes everywhere I go and gets me into trouble whenever she can. She makes me do terrible things."

Mrs. Jameson stared at me. "Who is this girl?" she asked. "Where does she come from? Why does she hate you?"

I looked into the corners again and peered into the shadows. Even though I couldn't see Elsie, I sensed her presence. She was nearby, watching and listening.

"Why are you looking in the corners?" she asked. "What do you expect to see?"

"Her," I whispered. "She could be anywhere."

Mrs. Jameson put her arm around me. "You're trembling, Annie."

"I'm so afraid of her."

"If you're in danger, you must tell someone."

"I've tried, but no one believes me. Dr. Benson says she's not real. He insists I imagine her. He claims I blame her for the bad things *I* do."

"Is she invisible to everyone but you?" Mrs. Jameson held me tighter.

A branch tapped against the window windowpane. Elsie stood outside peering at us through the glass. She made a hideous face when she saw me looking at her. "Not another word, Annie," she warned.

Mrs. Jameson looked at the window in alarm. "Why is it so dark out there?"

Elsie shook her head and pressed a finger to her lips. "I'm warning you. Don't tell that old lady anything."

"I have to leave," I said. "It's time for arts and crafts."

"No, stay — talk to me," Mrs. Jameson begged. "Let me help you."

Ignoring her, I left her in the library and ran down the hall.

Elsie ran beside me. "Stay away from that old lady," she whispered. "Don't talk to her. I won't allow you to have any friend but me."

She followed me into the arts and crafts room. Miss Ellis had set open jars of tempera paint on the tables. Some of the women were already painting winter scenes — children ice-skating or sledding. Snowmen. Snow-covered fir trees. Maybe I'd paint a ghost in a snowy graveyard, a crow for sorrow in a tree, an angel with a mean face, a broken sled. That would at least be original.

But before I had a chance to lift my brush, Elsie dipped her finger into a jar of red paint and wrote a bad word on my drawing paper. When I tried to take the jar away from her, I upset it and several others. In no time, a pool of various colors spread across the table, ruining pictures and dripping onto the floor. The women at my table hastened to move out of range of the paint, but most of them were spattered.

Not only did Miss Ellis blame me for the mess, but she accused me of laughing as if it were the best prank ever. It was Elsie who'd laughed, of course, but she'd made it sound like me. Defeated, I sat down at a small table in the corner and took the pencil Miss Ellis gave me.

"Draw a snow scene with that."

When I left the arts and crafts room, Elsie followed me to my private tutoring class where she made sure I failed every quiz. Speaking for me, she told Mr. French he was a lousy teacher. Like Miss Ellis, he said he'd report my behavior to Dr. Benson. Thanks to my so-called friend, I was doomed to be in trouble constantly.

After class, Elsie said, "See what happens when you talk to other people?"

Without answering, I went to my room and slammed the door in her face. Of course a shut door didn't keep Elsie from following me inside and taking her favorite perch on the curtain rod.

Imitating Mrs. Jameson, she said, "Oh, Annie, stay, talk to me, let me help you, you poor dear, sweet girl."

"I hate you," I muttered.

"Oh, boo-hoo-hoo. I thought we were friends. Am I mistaken, dear Annie?" She pretended to wipe tears from her eyes.

In desperation, I threw a book at her. It went right through her and broke the glass in my window.

Elsie pretended to be shocked. "Oh, my, that window will be hard to explain," she said, "but I suppose you'll blame me as usual. Not that anyone believes you. Your state of mind grows more precarious every day."

At that moment, my door flew open and Nurse O'Brien appeared. "What was that noise?"

"It was an accident," I said. "I thought there was a fly or something at the window and I tried to kill it with my book, but—"

By now the nurse was staring in shock at the broken glass on the floor. "Oh dear, oh dear," she said, "I don't understand. How could there be a fly in the winter?"

With a loud laugh, Elsie vanished into the night, and Nurse O'Brien stared at me. "How can you laugh about this?"

She left the room to fetch a handyman. He cleaned up the glass and covered the window with cardboard. "It'll be a bit cold in here," he said, "but I can't replace the glass until morning. Serves you right for busting it. A fly, my eye."

Next, Dr. Benson arrived. Obviously annoyed, he dropped a snow-covered math book on my desk. "You are not to blame this on Elsie. You must learn to take responsibility for your actions."

"I admit I threw a book at Elsie," I told him. "She got me into trouble, and I was mad."

"No," he said. "You got yourself into trouble, and you threw the book at the window, possibly at your own reflection, but not at Elsie."

He sighed and sat down in the rocking chair. "Mrs. Coakley complained about your rudeness at lunch. Miss Ellis reported an incident with tempera paint. Mr. French says you failed all your quizzes and then told him he was a bad teacher. After the wall incident, I expected better behavior today."

"I'm sorry you won't believe me. You have no idea what she's like."

"You'll have dinner in your room tonight. Without you and your unpredictable outbursts, the others might enjoy their meal."

He rose to his feet to leave, but paused at the door. "Please try to improve, Annie. You're a young girl. I don't want you to spend the rest of your childhood here."

I watched the door close behind him. A cold stream of air slipped through the cardboard taped to my window. Elsie settled herself on the wardrobe. "Tsk, tsk. What a bad, bad girl you are, Annie Browne."

I sat on my bed and silently hated her.

TWENTY

THE NEXT DAY, Mother and Father came for a visit. Dr. Benson was with them. From the looks on their faces, it was clear they'd heard about my behavior. I hoped they wouldn't notice the faint scribbles on the wall, but of course they did. Mother gasped and Father looked at me with sorrow.

"I didn't do it," I said.

Dr. Benson gestured to my parents to come closer. He spoke softly, but I heard him anyway. "All of this is due to Annie's guilt about Elsie. She'll need more treatment than I thought."

They nodded unhappily. Mother reached for Father's hand, and he clasped it tightly.

"Stop by and see me after visiting hours," Dr. Benson told them and left the three of us alone in my room.

Fortunately, the handyman had replaced the glass in my window before visiting hours, so I didn't need to explain why I'd thrown the book. But Father mentioned it anyway.

"Cedar Grove is billing us for the window you broke, as well as the paint for your room. Why on earth do you behave this way?"

"I don't remember," I lied. "I guess I was upset or something."

Father and Mother looked at each other with sorrowful faces.

"I'm sorry," I said. "I don't mean to make you unhappy. I just want to come home. I hate it here. Why can't you take me home? Don't you love me?" My voice rose like a child's. "Please take me home, please."

"Of course we love you." Mother embraced me. I smelled her perfume and shampoo, nice smells, familiar smells. I wanted to stay where I was forever. Surely I was safe from Elsie in her arms.

"Home isn't home without you," Father said, "but Dr. Benson is concerned about your state of mind. He insists you're not ready to leave Cedar Grove."

"If you'd just stop blaming Elsie," Mother added. "Neither your father nor I understand your obsession with her. You have nothing to feel guilty about. No one blames you for not being friends with her."

Their voices flowed over me. They meant to comfort me, but they didn't understand. They had no idea. Nothing I said would help.

The subject changed to the weather. "Such a long, cold winter we've had," Mother said. "If only spring would come."

"*The Evening Sun* says it's the coldest winter on record," Father said.

"I believe it," Mother said.

When we ran out of things to say about the weather, Father told me the people next door had gotten a dog from the pound.

"He's a cute little mutt, but he barks all day and all night. It's driving me crazy."

Mother told me Dickie Simmons fell through the ice on the lake, but his big brother Bobby saved him. Jane's mother and father went to New York to see a play on Broadway. She ran into Miss Harrison at the grocery store. "She asked about you, Annie. She misses you and hopes you come home soon."

By the time the visit ended, I was exhausted. It was as if I'd been making polite conversation with friendly strangers. Maybe Dr. Benson had told them not to say anything that might agitate me. Or disturb my precarious state of mind.

. . .

At noon, I took my seat beside Mrs. Jameson in the dining room. Before I touched my soup, I spotted Elsie in a tree near the window, hurling snowballs at two men shoveling wind-blown snow from the sidewalks. She had a remarkably good aim. The men were obviously puzzled and angry, but saw no one to blame.

Mrs. Jameson touched my hand to get my attention. "What are you looking at, Annie?"

My whole body stiffened in alarm. "Nothing."

Mrs. Jameson continued to stare at the tree. "It's like the shadow in the library yesterday," she said. "I can't see what's causing it. Are you sure you don't see it?"

When I shook my head, she pointed directly at Elsie. "It's right there in those branches."

Elsie saw us looking and scowled. Like yesterday, she pressed her finger to her mouth and shook her head. With an agility she'd never had in real life, she jumped from the tree and ran across the snow toward the pond.

Losing sight of her among the trees, I turned to Mrs. Jameson.

"That's funny," she said. "The shadow's gone. It just floated away."

She picked up her spoon and began to eat her soup. "Too salty by half," she said, "but edible."

After lunch, Mrs. Jameson said, "We need to talk, Annie. Those shadows are bothering me. I believe you know more about them than you're saying."

"I can't talk now." I edged away from her. "I have homework to do."

She took my arm. "Come with me. It's important."

I let her lead me to the library. What did she think I knew? What did she suspect?

I chose a different couch with no window view. Perhaps Elsie wouldn't see us here.

"Something was in that tree," Mrs. Jameson said in a low voice. "A patch of darkness, vague, unformed. I couldn't make out what it was, but I know it was there." She paused and took my hand. "And I know it has something to do with you, Annie."

"No, you're wrong." I told her. "There was nothing in the tree except a crow. I was looking at a crow, that's all."

"There was no crow, Annie." She squeezed my hand. "Why won't you confide in me? Don't you trust me?"

No, I didn't trust Mrs. Jameson enough to tell her about Elsie. Look what happened when I tried to explain what I saw — I was called a liar, delusional, guilt ridden. Elsie was a figment of my imagination. She wasn't real.

If I told Mrs. Jameson a ghost had been sitting in the

tree, throwing snowballs, she too would think I was crazy. I'd lose the only friend I'd made in Cedar Grove.

"Please tell me what's frightening you so."

I looked into her eyes and saw only sympathy. Taking a deep breath, I decided to take a chance. If one person, just one, believed me maybe I wouldn't feel so alone. "Do you believe in ghosts?"

"Oh, yes," she said. "Most definitely."

My heart beat faster. "Have you actually seen one?"

"This must be a secret between you and me," she said. "Promise not to tell Dr. Benson. He already thinks I'm delusional."

I crossed my heart and promised.

She paused, perhaps to think, before beginning. "I saw my first ghost when I was a small child — three or four years old at the most. My grandmother died before I was born, but she often visited me. She'd sit by my bed at night when I was afraid of the dark and sing lullabies to comfort me."

"Did you tell your mother and father about her?"

"Oh, yes, several times. I even described the flowered dress she wore and her white hair, but they always dismissed it as a dream. As you already know, most people simply refuse to believe in ghosts."

"Did you ever see a scary ghost?"

"When I was younger—not young like you, but younger than I am now—I stayed in haunted inns and hotels and wrote stories about my experiences. I published them in magazines that go for that sort of thing."

She paused a moment as if she were remembering those days. "Usually the ghosts were sad and lonely. I found ways to help them leave this world and move on to a better place. A little nudge was all most of them needed."

She frowned. "But once in a while, I encountered vengeful spirits who'd been wronged when they were alive. They were angry. They hungered to get even with their enemies but often ended up taking out their rage on any hapless mortal who crossed their path. Occasionally I helped them find peace, but the really troubled ones always resisted."

"You must have been very brave."

Mrs. Jameson laughed. "I must confess I once fled from a hotel in the middle of the night. I'd never felt such an evil presence. It was as if I were being suffocated. I feared for my sanity and maybe even my life."

She readjusted her glasses on the bridge of her nose and said, "Tell me about your ghost, Annie."

"Her name is Elsie Schneider," I began. "She died of the flu last November. She wanted to be my friend while she was alive, but I didn't like her. Now that she's dead, she says

I must be her friend, but I hate her more now than I did before she died. She's ruined my whole life. Can you make her go away and leave me alone?"

"What was she like before she died?"

Starting with Elsie's first visit to my house, I told Mrs. Jameson everything: how I became friends with Rosie and dropped Elsie, how we teased her in the park and stole her flu mask, how she died, how I crashed my sled into her grave and woke her up.

"Ever since then, she's followed me everywhere I go," I said. "She turned my friends against me, she made me say terrible things and do awful things. She's jealous and angry and hateful. She wants everything I have, even my parents."

I looked at Mrs. Jameson, desperate for her help. "Please tell me you can send her where she belongs."

A noise drew our attention to a dark corner. Elsie stood there, barely visible in the shadows, watching Mrs. Jameson and me.

"She's in that corner." Mrs. Jameson clasped my hand. "I can't see her, but I feel her. She's angry, isn't she?"

I drew closer to Mrs. Jameson. "She doesn't want me to have any friend except her."

"I sense that." She continued to stare at Elsie. "I see her outline now," she whispered.

Elsie's face twisted into a grimace of hate. "You'll be sorry, Annie!" With that, she disappeared.

"She's gone, isn't she?" Mrs. Jameson asked. "For a second I saw her as clearly as I see you, and then poof, she vanished like a magician's trick."

"Elsie's good at disappearing, but she's even better at reappearing." I clung to Mrs. Jameson for a moment. "Don't worry. We'll both see her again."

"Elsie's a very troubled child. Angry and vengeful. I'll do all I can to help you, but I'm not as strong as I once was. It may be more than I can do, Annie."

"Please be careful," I told her. "Elsie might try to hurt you."

We walked to the door together. "Don't worry about me, Annie. I've dealt with spirits worse than Elsie. After all, she's just a little girl."

I left Mrs. Jameson reluctantly. I was already late for arts and crafts, but instead of hurrying, I walked slowly, directing all my mental energy at Elsie. *Please please please, do not hurt Mrs. Jameson. Please please please, do not hurt Mrs. Jameson.* Over and over again, over and over again, I repeated my plea until the words ran together and made no sense.

TWENTY-ONE

I DIDN'T SEE ELSIE AGAIN until just before dinner. While I was combing my hair, she came through the window and sat on top of the wardrobe. The smirk on her face disturbed me. She'd either done something already or was about to do it. Whatever it was, it would bring me grief.

"Where have you been?" I asked her.

She shrugged and kicked the wardrobe door with her heels. "Oh, just out and about, fooling with this and that, nothing to write home about."

"You've done something. I can tell."

"Well, aren't you a clever girl?" She swung her heels so hard the wardrobe vibrated.

"Tell me."

"It's my secret, but don't worry — you'll find out soon enough." Elsie took a flying leap from the wardrobe and landed on my bed. She bounced a couple of times. "Just remember, it's your fault, Annie. If you'd do what I tell you, I'd be good all the time."

"If you've hurt Mrs. Jameson, I'll—"

"You'll what?" She laughed and vanished, leaving me even more worried than before. I drew my breath in and out, in and out, and struggled to control my fear. What had she done?

The dinner bell interrupted my thoughts. Filled with dread of what I might learn, I walked down the hall slowly. When I was close enough to hear voices and smell food, I stopped, closed my eyes tightly, and whispered, "Please let Mrs. Jameson be at the table, please let her be all right."

"What are you doing standing there with your eyes shut?" Nurse Baker bustled up to me and gave me a push through the door. "Take your seat at the table. Don't keep the others waiting."

The first thing I saw was Mrs. Jameson's empty chair. I sat down in my seat and watched the door. At any moment, I'd see her enter the dining room. She was late, that's all it was.

Elsie appeared at the window. Her smile revealed her

crooked teeth, browner now than before. I sank into my seat. What had she done? Where was Mrs. Jameson?

Outside the window, Elsie laughed.

As the servers entered with trays of food, I leaned across the table and caught Miss Nelson's attention. She was a small, thin, nervous woman who seemed afraid of me and my strange outbursts, but she had a kind face.

"Excuse me, but do you know where Mrs. Jameson is?"

Miss Nelson blinked several times, but instead of answering, she turned to Mrs. Coakley, who looked at me as if I'd asked a rude question.

"I can't think *why* you would care," she said in a low voice, "but Mrs. Jameson is in the infirmary. She had a bad fall and broke her hip." Looking at me, she added, "Some people say she was *pushed*."

Without another word, she turned her attention to her dinner and began cutting her meat and vegetables into tiny pieces.

Miss Nelson leaned across the table, her eyes moist. "When you're her age and you break your hip, it's the beginning of the end. Mark my words, she'll be in bed the rest of her life."

Mrs. Coakley looked sharply at Miss Nelson. "Now, Edith, don't get yourself all het up."

My appetite gone, I left the table and ran out of the dining room. The other patients watched me go. *Annie Browne, the crazy girl. Better stay away from her. No telling what she'll do next. Throw something, bite you, insult you, stab you with her butter knife.*

Nurse Calloway caught up with me in the hall. "You haven't finished your dinner, Annie."

"Please, I don't feel well. May I go to my room?"

Nurse Baker would have sent me back to the dining room, but Nurse Calloway said, "Yes, of course, Annie. I hope you feel better in the morning. If you want soup, I can send it to your room."

"Thank you, but I'm not hungry."

I trudged down the hall. Elsie had made Mrs. Jameson fall. There was no doubt in my mind. That was her secret. That was what she'd gloated about. She'd hurt the only person who believed me, the only one who might help me.

I sat on my bed and wrapped myself in an afghan Mother had crocheted for me. The clock on my bureau ticked, each second loud in the silence. The wind pounded on my window, and the trees bowed and bent as it passed through their branches.

I pictured Mrs. Jameson in the infirmary, listening to the same wind I heard. I hoped she wasn't in pain. Perhaps

Mrs. Coakley was wrong about the fall. Maybe Mrs. Jameson was just bruised, and she'd be at breakfast or lunch tomorrow, and we'd go to the library and make plans.

A creaking noise drew my attention to the rocking chair. Elsie sat there, grinning.

I flung myself at her in fury. The rocking chair crashed to the floor, taking me with it, but Elsie slipped out of my hands and perched on the curtain rod safely out of my reach.

"How could you do it?" I screamed. "She never harmed you."

"I don't know what you're talking about. I swear you get crazier every day, Annie Browne. They'll be taking you to the lunatic asylum any day now. I hear they have a nice padded cell and a straitjacket all ready for you."

"Don't lie to me. You know exactly what I'm talking about. Mrs. Jameson is in the infirmary with a broken hip because you made her fall down the steps."

"Oh, that old lady." Elsie shrugged to show she couldn't care less about Mrs. Jameson. "It's your fault she fell, not mine. I warned you not to make friends with anyone. We don't need an old biddy coming between us, so I took care of her."

In a rage, I lunged at the curtains and tried to pull her down, but Elsie scurried to the top of the wardrobe before I could catch her.

She laughed. "You can't catch me, I'm the gingerbread man."

I stood there panting in frustration, my fists clenched. "I hate you, I despise you, I abhor you, I detest you," I shouted. "I'd kill you all over again if I could!"

Elsie sneered. "You'd better watch what you say to me, or I'll make it look like *you* pushed Mrs. Jameson down the steps. I can do that, you know."

I collapsed on my bed. If Dr. Benson believed I'd pushed Mrs. Jameson, they'd take me away in a straitjacket. Elsie would make sure I stayed there for the rest of my life.

"Well?" Elsie asked. "Are we friends now? Or must I make it look like you pushed the old lady, your so-called friend, down the steps?"

I forced myself to stare into her eyes. Death itself must look like Elsie, I thought. "Friends," I repeated. "You don't know how to be friends."

Elsie bared her crooked teeth like a dog about to bite. "How am I supposed to know? I never had a friend, remember? You should be good at it — but you're worse than I am. Look at the way you've treated me."

She paused to push her tangled hair out of her face. "You were my friend for a few days, but I got sick and Rosie turned you against me. And then you and your new friends ganged up on me in the park and Rosie stole my flu mask. And then I died! Not you. Not Rosie or any of those other girls. None of *you* died. Just me. *Me,* poor Elsie Schneider, the girl nobody liked. Couldn't you at least be sorry?"

"How many times must tell you? I'm sorry you died. There — does that satisfy you?"

"The only reason you're sorry," Elsie said, "is because you're stuck with me. I wouldn't be here if you'd treated me better."

"Oh, why can't you understand?" I clenched my fists to keep from slapping her. "You don't belong here anymore. You're dead, Elsie! You're dead, dead, DEAD!"

The walls rang with my words, which echoed and bounced like hard rubber balls caroming from chairs to tables to bureaus. *Dead, dead, DEAD. Dead, dead, DEAD.* I covered my ears, but the word rang in my head. *Dead, dead, DEAD!*

I shut my eyes and waited for Elsie to say something. To scream at me. To throw things. After a few moments of total silence, I opened my eyes, but I didn't see her. "Are you still here?"

In a cold voice from the top of the wardrobe, Elsie said, "Of course, I'm still here. Where else would I be?"

In your grave like a normal dead person, I thought.

I got into bed and turned my back on her. I wanted to go home. I wanted my life back — the way it was before the park, before the viewing, before my sled ride in the cemetery.

But most of all, I wanted to be rid of Elsie.

TWENTY-TWO

DAYS PASSED WITH NO WORD from Mrs. Jameson. I heard Mrs. Coakley tell Miss Nelson she was doing poorly and might be transferred to a nursing home. I asked Dr. Benson about her, but he simply said she was doing as well as expected. Whatever that meant.

Elsie had her own stories about Mrs. Jameson. "I went to the infirmary," she told me. "I saw that old lady who fell down the steps. She's going to die, Annie, I'm certain of it."

I told myself not to believe anything Elsie said. She was a liar, I knew that. But I was scared she might do something to make Mrs. Jameson worse.

After a week of misery, fear, and worry, I was finally allowed to visit Mrs. Jameson. At the door to the infirmary, Nurse Ryan stopped me.

"I can't allow you to stay more than fifteen minutes," she told me. "Mrs. Jameson is still weak and tires easily. She had a very bad fall, you know. It's a miracle she's still with us."

She studied my face for a moment. "She's quite fond of you, Annie." As she spoke, her own face looked puzzled, as if she couldn't imagine why Mrs. Jameson took any interest in a crazy girl like me. "She'll be happy to see you."

As quietly as possible, I followed the nurse down a narrow corridor between two rows of beds. The people were all old. Most of them were asleep, but a few raised their heads to watch me go by. I tried to smile at them, but they scared me. They were small and thin, like children old before their time. They looked as if they were waiting for something to happen, but they didn't know if it would be good or bad.

Mrs. Jameson was asleep in the last bed in the row. I didn't want to wake her, so I sat quietly in a wooden chair beside her. She breathed loudly, as if it took all her strength to inhale and exhale.

What if Miss Nelson was right? What if Mrs. Jameson never got out of that bed? Worse yet, what if Elsie was right and Mrs. Jameson died? My chest tightened with sorrow, which soon turned to anger.

Elsie had done this; she'd put Mrs. Jameson in this bed. She was a cruel and hateful spirit. We had to get rid of her.

I felt a touch on my hand and looked up to see Mrs. Jameson smiling at me. "Oh, it's good to see you, Annie. I've been so worried about you." Her voice was so low, I had to lean close to hear her.

"I'm so sorry Elsie made you fall."

"Please don't blame yourself, Annie. It's not your fault."

"Yes, it is. If I'd been her friend while she was alive, maybe she'd be in her grave where she belongs."

Mrs. Jameson gazed at me in silence. Finally she said, "Suppose you try to be her friend now?"

I stared at her in disbelief. "I hate her! How can I be her friend? After all the horrible things she's done?"

"It won't be easy, but it might help Elsie move on and leave you in peace." She patted my hand. "Surely it's worth a try."

I closed my eyes for a moment and tried to calm down. The very idea repulsed me, but if it was the only way to rid myself of Elsie, I'd make myself do it. After all, Mrs. Jameson knew more about ghosts than I did.

I sniffed and blew my nose. "I'll try."

"Good girl." She smiled and squeezed my hand. "Come back tomorrow and tell me what happens."

Nurse Ryan tapped my shoulder. "Let her rest now. She's tired."

I leaned over and kissed Mrs. Jameson's cheek, but her eyes had already closed.

Before I left the infirmary, I looked at the nurse. "She's getting better, isn't she?"

Nurse Ryan began to go through a pile of paper on her desk. "Run along, Annie. Can't you see I have work to do?"

She hadn't answered my question, but it was probably because she was busy. I lingered a moment, just in case she had something else to say, but she kept her head down and ignored me.

I walked slowly back to my room, trying not to worry about Mrs. Jameson. It took older people longer to get well. I'd heard my mother say that when Grandmother was sick. She'd be all right in a few days, maybe a week.

What I needed to do now was take her advice. Maybe if I were Elsie's friend just for a little while, she'd be happy and go wherever dead people went. Then my life would return to normal — though, honestly, I wasn't sure I remembered normal.

Elsie met me in the doorway of my room. She'd pulled the covers off my bed and torn up the homework I'd spent hours doing.

"You went to see that crazy old lady, didn't you?"

"She's not crazy —"

"Crazy or not, I can make her have another accident, you know."

"No, please don't hurt her again. She's on your side. She wants us to be friends."

"I bet she does."

"Honestly, Elsie. She has a lot of sympathy for you."

"Ha." Elsie scowled in disbelief. "You're such a liar."

"I'm not lying. She wants me to be your friend. She wants me to make up for the way I treated you."

"That might be what *she* wants, but what about you, Annie?" She stared at me through narrowed eyes. "What do *you* want?"

"It's what I want, too. Mrs. Jameson convinced me I owe it to you."

"You better mean it, Annie Browne. If you're lying, I'll find out."

Doing my best to speak in a steady, truthful voice, I said, "Cross my heart and hope to die, if I ever tell a lie."

"So," she said. "Will we be bosom buddies just like girls in books?"

"Yes, of course, Elsie. Whatever you say."

"Best friends for all eternity. You and me. Just the two of us."

"Yes, yes, just you and me. Best friends for all eternity."
I had to struggle not to choke on *eternity*.

Elsie smiled. "I'm glad you finally see things my way." She looked around the room. "I'm sorry I tore up your homework. You'll have to do it over again, I guess. I'd do it for you, but I don't remember how to do math anymore."

As she tidied up my room, I opened my math book and redid my homework. I hoped my promise would protect Mrs. Jameson, but I wasn't sure I'd be rid of Elsie anytime soon. *Best friends for all eternity* — those words made me fear she meant to be around for a long time.

From then on, I visited Mrs. Jameson whenever I could. Elsie often followed me and watched from the door. She didn't like my spending so much time with Mrs. Jameson, but as long as I was nice to her, she had no reason to make a scene.

Sometimes I'd find Mrs. Jameson propped up on pillows, either crocheting or reading *The Pickwick Papers,* one of the few Dickens novels she hadn't read. Often she was asleep, and I'd sit beside her and wait for her to wake up. She still breathed heavily, and she'd developed a bad cough.

She always asked about Elsie. "Is she happier?"

"I guess so," I'd say. "At least she's stopped getting me into trouble."

"And how do you feel?"

"Not too bad, but I hope she leaves soon. It's hard to pretend to like her."

"Well, keep on pretending, Annie. Your efforts will be rewarded, I'm sure."

Before I left, she asked me to read *The Pickwick Papers* to her. Her eyes were weak, she said, and it tired her to read. We both laughed at Mr. Pickwick's antics. He was such a silly man, but sweet and charming. We couldn't help liking him even when he made mistakes.

That afternoon, Dr. Benson said, "You've had no bad reports this week, not even from Nurse Baker. You're doing well in your calisthenics class. Miss Hyde tells me you've improved your strength and can do twenty or so sit-ups now. You've been well behaved in arts and crafts. Mr. French is pleased that your schoolwork has improved. The staff feels you're finally learning to control your behavior."

He smiled at me. "If you continue like this, Annie, you might be allowed to go home in a few weeks."

I skipped all the way to my room. Home. I'd soon go home!

Elsie looked up when I opened the door. She was sitting

on the carpet playing with a set of paper dolls. Although I seldom played with paper dolls, Elsie had begged me to ask Mother to bring some. She had never had any of her own. She played with them for hours, drawing clothes and making up stories about them — which I never heard because she whispered them to herself. I had a feeling I didn't want to know the plots.

"Guess what?" I asked. "Dr. Benson says I can go home soon."

Elsie clapped her hands. "Oh, Annie, how wonderful! We'll have so much fun at your house."

I clenched my teeth to keep from saying, *No, no, you aren't coming with me, you're going wherever dead people go.* But I knew better. A response like that would enrage Elsie. So, forcing myself to smile, I pretended to be as happy as she was.

"Just me and you," Elsie went on. "We'll go everywhere together. We'll share everything. We won't need anyone else."

"But sometimes I might go to Jane's house to play —"

"No you won't," Elsie interrupted. "What do you need Jane for? *I'm* your friend, your only friend, your best friend, your *true* friend." She scowled at me. "And you better not forget it!"

No, I wouldn't forget. How could I? She'd be with me every day and every night, watching me, making sure I had no friends but her.

"It's Rosie's fault we weren't friends before I died," Elsie said. "She turned everyone against me, including you. She stole my flu mask because she wanted me to die. I know it for a fact."

"Can't you just forget what Rosie said and did? You bring it up over and over again. Honestly, I'm tired of hearing it. We're friends now."

Elsie scowled. "I never forget anything." Snatching up my favorite paper doll, she glared at its smiling face and red hair. "This one looks like Rosie. Don't you hate her?" Giving me a sly look, she ripped the doll's head off.

I tried to rescue the poor thing, but Elsie wadded the two pieces into a ball and threw it across the room. I watched it roll under the wardrobe.

Elsie moved closer to me. When she opened her mouth to speak, I noticed that two or three of her teeth had fallen out. She was changing. Her skin had gotten dry and flaky, and her hair hung in tangled knots. I backed away from her, but she scooted across the carpet, keeping as close to me as possible.

"Listen, Annie. I'm getting even with Rosie, just you wait. And the others too." She gathered up all the paper dolls and decapitated them one by one. Mother, father, sister, brother, and baby, all drifted to the floor. Heads here, bodies there. It was a massacre. "They'll all be sorry they were mean to me."

While I sat there speechless, Elsie went on, "You and I will give Rosie a taste of her own medicine. I've got it all planned. We'll get some rat poison and put it in her lemonade. She'll drink it and — ha ha — that's the end of her."

"You can't do something like that!"

"Oh, yes, I can. And you're going to help me!"

"You must be insane — I'll never help you do something that horrible to my friend!"

"You're *my* friend now, not Rosie's. Of course you'll help me." She grinned, and another tooth fell out of her mouth. It landed on the carpet among the headless paper dolls. She scooped it up and slipped it into her pocket as if nothing had happened.

"I won't — you can't make me!"

"Ha. I can make you do anything I want. You'll see!" Elsie laughed and darted out the door. I hurried after her, but she'd already disappeared.

Fearing she might be on her way to Mrs. Jameson, I ran to the infirmary.

When she saw me, Nurse Ryan frowned. "You again," she said. "Fifteen minutes, no more."

Mrs. Jameson was propped up on pillows, looking out the window beside her bed.

She smiled when she saw me and beckoned me closer. "Spring is coming at last," she said. "The edges of the trees are softening, and I see hints of green and yellow and pink in their branches."

I pressed my face against the glass so I could see the ground beneath the window. "The snow is melting and the daffodils are blooming in the garden," I told her.

"My favorite flowers," she said. "I love their frilly little bonnets."

I sat in the chair by the bed and held her hand. "How do you feel today?"

"Oh, about the same." She coughed, and I filled a glass of water for her.

After taking a few sips, she said, "I've been thinking about you and Elsie. Has anything changed?"

"For the worse," I said, "not the better. When Dr. Benson sends me home, she means to come with me. I'm supposed to help her poison Rosie. She can't make me do something like that, can she?"

Mrs. Jameson looked at me huddled in the chair, probably a picture of misery. "Of course not. No one can make you do something you don't want to do."

"'That's what *she* thinks." On silent feet, Elsie had appeared beside me.

"What are you doing here?" I whispered.

"I don't trust you, Annie. You're plotting against me."

Mrs. Jameson looked straight at Elsie. "That's not true. We want to help you. Poor child, you're so unhappy."

"Stop staring at me," Elsie said. "You can't see me. You can't hear me either. No one can, unless I want them to."

"I can both see and hear you," Mrs. Jameson said. "You're standing right there beside Annie."

"Liar," Elsie said. "I bet you can't tell me what I look like."

"You're wearing a ragged blue dress with a lace collar and a pale blue sash," Mrs. Jameson said. "You have no shoes or socks. Your hair is long and blond and in need of a good combing. Your face is pale and very sad."

"I'm not sad— don't you dare say I am. I have a friend now, and I'm going to get my way and do what I want and have fun." Elsie glared at Mrs. Jameson. "And you can't stop me!"

"You're angry now, aren't you?"

"You'd make anybody angry, you crazy old lady."

"Come sit beside me, Elsie. Let me comfort you." Mrs. Jameson stretched out her arms as if to embrace Elsie.

Quick as a cat, Elsie moved out of her reach. "You want to send me back to my grave, *that's* what you want to do, but I don't like it there. I'm staying here with Annie. I have plans. And she's helping me whether she likes it or not."

"Those plans won't make you happy, Elsie."

"If you don't leave me alone, I'll make something worse happen to you!"

Elsie disappeared as quickly and quietly as she'd appeared, but a chill remained in the room, and her words rang in my head.

I turned to Mrs. Jameson in despair. "Tell me what to do."

She reached for my hand. "Be kind to her, earn her trust. I'll help you if I'm able."

I stroked her hands. They were thinner now, and the veins stuck out in knotted blue ropes. "When you're well and strong," I told her, "you'll think of something."

She sighed. "When I was younger, I'd have made her listen, I'd have won her trust, but I failed to reach her." She lay back against her pillows. "Oh, Annie, that poor child doesn't know what she wants or where to go. I feel so useless."

When she began coughing again, I helped her sip from the glass of water. Her eyes were far away, and her face was as sad as Elsie's.

After she'd drunk what she wanted, I put the glass on the table by her bed. "Do you want me to read to you?"

She closed her eyes. "I'm a bit tired, Annie. I'd probably fall asleep before you read the first sentence."

I sat beside her and watched her go to sleep. "Please get well," I whispered and kissed her forehead. Her skin was warm, and her face was flushed. She probably had a fever. And a bad cough. Maybe she had bronchitis. I'd had it several times when I was little, and I remembered the fever and the terrible cough. Another week or two, and she'd be fine.

Nurse Ryan tapped my shoulder. "Time's up, Annie."

At the infirmary door, I wanted to ask Nurse Ryan if Mrs. Jameson had bronchitis, but she'd already started going through the endless piles of paper on her desk. I left without bothering her. What was the use? She wouldn't tell me anything.

TWENTY-THREE

ELSIE POUNCED ON ME from a shadowy corner in the hall. "Blabbermouth," she said. "You promised not to tell that old lady about me."

"I didn't have to tell her — she saw you, Elsie."

"No, she didn't. She tricked me, and you helped her. What kind of friend are you?"

"Why won't you believe me? Mrs. Jameson sees ghosts. She has a gift."

"Some gift."

"She wants to help you, Elsie."

"She wants to help *you,* not me, but she can't make me go anywhere, and neither can you. I'm staying right here!"

With that, Elsie darted away. Behind me, Nurse Ryan called, "Who are you talking to, Annie?"

"Nobody!" Turning my back on her, I ran down the steps.

Before going to my room, I stopped in the library to look for a book. I hadn't been there five minutes before Elsie joined me.

"Find something good," she said. "I want you to read to me like you read to that old lady."

"Read to yourself," I muttered. "You don't need me to do it."

"Words don't make sense anymore," she said. "The letters turn into squiggles and fall off the pages. It's a good thing I don't have to go to school."

She sounded so sad, I almost felt sorry for her. "What do you want me to read?"

"I don't know." She ran her finger lightly up and down the spines of the books. "Are there any stories about graveyards and dead people and what happens to them after they're buried?"

Startled by her choice of subject, I shook my head.

"How about ghosts? You must know some ghost stories." Her eyes mocked me. "Maybe you don't like ghosts. Maybe they scare you."

She laughed and swept along the shelves, picking books at random and throwing them on the floor. I scurried behind her, picking them up almost as fast as she threw them down.

"Stop it," I begged. "You'll get me into trouble."

She threw *The Pickwick Papers* at me. "Look what I found. The same book you're reading to that old lady. I want you to read it to me!"

The book flew at my face, its pages flapping like a bird's wings. I ducked, and it thudded to the floor just as the librarian poked her head around the shelves to see what was going on.

"What was that noise?" she asked me. "How did this book get on the floor?"

I scooped up *The Pickwick Papers*. "I'm sorry," I stammered. "I dropped it."

She looked suspicious, but she checked the book out for me. "It's due in two weeks, Annie. Make sure you return it in good condition."

I thanked her and left the library.

"That was a close call." Elsie reappeared in the hall. "I was hoping you'd get in trouble again."

Once we were in the safety of my room, Elsie insisted I read the first chapter of *The Pickwick Papers*.

"I don't think you'll like it," I told her.

"If you and that old lady like it, why wouldn't I like it?"

"It's just that it's kind of old-fashioned in the beginning. It gets better, but—"

Elsie opened the book to the first page. "Read it. If I don't like it, I'll tell you."

I cleared my throat and began to read chapter one:

The first ray of light which illumines the gloom, and converts into a dazzling brilliancy that obscurity in which the earlier history of the public career of the immortal Pickwick would appear to be involved—

Before I'd reached the end of the first paragraph, Elsie snatched the book away and looked at the page in disbelief.

"What's this story about? It doesn't make sense."

"Well, it's about Mr. Pickwick and his friends. They belong to a club, and they travel around and do funny things."

"You and the old lady like this book? You think it's funny?"

"I told you it's old-fashioned. You have to be patient."

Elsie threw the book across the room. For a moment, I feared it would go through the window, but this time it landed on the floor.

"You don't want me to keep reading?"

"No. That book bores me to death." She laughed. With her mouth wide open, I saw she'd lost another tooth. *"Bores me to death —* that's a good joke. You bore me to death, too. So does that old lady and everybody else in this place. I can't wait to go to your house and have fun."

The next day, my parents came to visit. From the top of the wardrobe, Elsie watched me run to Mother. Elsie had an odd expression on her face — some anger, some envy, some sorrow, all mixed up together.

"You look so pretty today," I told Mother. "I love that blue sweater. Your pearls go so well with it." I looked over her shoulder at Elsie and sent a message from my mind to hers. *She's my mother, not yours. She loves me, not you.*

"Why, thank you, Annie." Mother hugged me.

The wardrobe creaked. Elsie sighed and sent a stream of cold air across the room. Mother shivered.

"Your room's an icebox," she said. "It's warmer outside than it is in here."

I grabbed her hand. "Let's go for a walk. It's too nice to stay inside."

Father smiled. "What a good idea, Annie. I saw the first daffodils this morning."

Mother kept my hand in hers, and Father took my other

hand. Linked, we walked out of the building. I glanced behind us. Elsie followed, smiling as if she had a secret.

"Oh, no." Mother came to a stop and stared at the garden. "Who would do something so dreadful?"

Feeling sick, I looked at the daffodils. All of their pretty yellow heads lay scattered in the dirt. I was glad Mrs. Jameson wasn't there to see it.

I glanced at Elsie. She made scissor motions with her fingers. "Snip snip — off with their heads."

"What did you say, Annie?" Father asked.

"Nothing."

He looked at me, but Mother hadn't heard Elsie. She was down on her knees gathering the flower heads as if she thought she could stick them back on their stalks.

Father spoke to me in a low voice. "I could have sworn you made some sort of joke."

"I don't know what you heard, but you're wrong," I told him. "I'm as sad about the daffodils as you and Mother. I can't imagine a person in their right mind doing something like this."

I looked behind him. Elsie stuck out her tongue and swung on a tree limb. "*I'm* not the crazy one," she said.

With a sigh, Father bent down to help Mother to her feet. "There's nothing you can do about the daffodils, Ida."

She held up a handful of flowers. "I can at least take

these to the office and show them to the director. Perhaps he'll find the culprit."

Elsie sniggered, and Father looked at me again. "Did I hear you laugh?"

I tried my best not to look as hurt as I felt. "No, Father. There's nothing funny about dead flowers."

He looked at me, his eyes full of doubt, and turned away. Neither he nor Mother took my hand. I walked behind them with Elsie at my heels, snipping at my hair with imaginary scissors.

"They don't love you anymore," she whispered. "I go to your house at night when they're in bed, and I listen to what they say. They want Dr. Benson to send you to the loony bin."

I pressed my fingers into my ears. "Liar!"

Mother looked back, her face alarmed, but Father took her arm and whispered something to her.

"See?" Elsie said. "He's telling her it's just another one of your insane outbursts. They're so tired of dealing with your craziness. The loony bin's the place for you, Annie Browne."

I hurried to catch up with my parents, but they walked on as if they'd forgotten I was there. Elsie stuck to my side.

"They think *you* killed the flowers," she said. "That's

why they're going to see the director. They intend to tell him you destroyed the garden. And then — poof! Off to the loony bin!"

It wasn't true. My parents loved me. They'd never send me to an insane asylum. *Liar, liar, liar,* I muttered in a voice too low for anyone to hear.

In the office, Mother showed the ruined flowers to Mr. Owens, the director. "Whoever did this should be disciplined."

"Is every flower cut?" he asked.

"Yes," Father said. "Someone destroyed the garden."

Mr. Owens watched Mother drop the flowers on his desk. "Could it be the work of an animal?" he asked. "A groundhog perhaps?"

"I don't think so," Father said.

"Absolutely not," Mother said at the same time.

"Well," Mr. Owens said, "thank you for telling me. I'll look into the matter. We spend quite a bit to keep our grounds beautiful."

After we left the office, I grabbed Father's hand. "I didn't ruin the garden," I told him. "I didn't!"

Mother and Father looked at me in surprise. "Of course you didn't," Father said. "Whoever said you did?"

"It was —" I stopped myself just in time. If I blamed

Elsie, they'd be certain I'd done it. "It was the way the director looked at me. Didn't you notice?"

Mother hugged me. "Please don't worry about it, darling."

I held her tightly. "Do you still love me?"

"Of course I do."

"And Father, do you?"

He held my shoulders and looked into my eyes. "Annie, where do you get these notions? We both love you very much, and we're longing for you to come home."

From the shadows, Elsie taunted me. "They're lying. They don't love you. They don't want you to come home."

I put my fingers in my ears to deafen myself, but I heard her anyway. Her lies were in my head. Her words circled endlessly, full of hatred, tormenting me.

Father put his arm around my shoulders. "I know you don't like it here, but soon you'll be home and all of this will be forgotten."

Mother wiped my eyes with her handkerchief. "Don't cry, darling. We'll be back tomorrow."

I watched them walk away. *No, Father,* I thought, *this will never be forgotten.*

When I returned to my room, Elsie was waiting for me. "Why did you destroy the daffodils?"

She shrugged. "It was fun snip-snip-snipping their heads off."

"No. You did it to hurt Mrs. Jameson."

"Oh, boo-hoo-hoo," Elsie wept. "Bad me. I killed the old lady's favorite flowers. Their dear little frilly bonnets are scattered all over the grass. That's just so, so sad."

With a laugh, Elsie ducked away from me and settled herself in the rocking chair. "The old lady's trying to take you away from me. But I won't let her. If she's not careful, she'll fall out of bed and crack her head."

"Please don't hurt her."

Elsie narrowed her eyes and examined my face. "Who do you like most, me or that old lady? Don't lie. I'll know if you do."

I forced myself not to turn my head away. "I like you both the same."

"What if you were in a boat going down the river and it started to sink and you could only save one of us? Would you choose me or her?"

"You're already dead."

"No, this is pretend. I'm alive, and so is she. Which one, Annie? Which one? Me or her?"

"You, Elsie," I lied. "I'd choose you."

She rocked back and forth so fast her edges blurred. "You're lying," she said.

"No, no, I'd never lie to you. Friends always tell each other the truth."

Elsie stopped rocking and sighed. "Why did that old lady say I looked sad? Do you think I do?"

"Sometimes."

Elsie smoothed the skirt of her dress over her bony knees. "Are you sad sometimes?"

"Yes. Everybody is."

"Even Rosie?"

"Even Rosie."

She began rocking again, slowly this time. My room was so quiet I heard the woman in the room next to mine cough. Someone walked past my door. The floor overhead creaked.

I came a little closer. "What are you sad about, Elsie?"

"I have lots to be sad about," she said. "Much more than either you or Rosie or anyone else. For one thing, I'm dead, which isn't much fun, if you really want to know. For another, you aren't really my friend. I'm not as smart as I used to be, but I know you hate me. You hated me when I was alive, and you hate me even more now!"

Her voice was rising and I knew she was getting angry, so I tried to tell her it wasn't true, I was her friend, but she kept yelling.

"Here's the saddest thing of all. My mother is dead. But your mother is alive, Rosie's mother is alive, Lucy, Jane, Eunice — every one of you have mothers who love you. But not me!"

She began to rock so fast I expected the chair to fall over backward or break into pieces. Her tangled hair flew around her face, her bony hands gripped the chair's arms. In a moment, her mood had changed from sorrow to rage.

"I hate you, Annie!" she screamed. "I don't want to be your friend after all."

"Fine," I yelled. "I don't want to be your friend."

"You won't be that old lady's friend either. I'll see to that."

She jumped from the rocking chair and ran toward my door. I tried to stop her, but she blocked my path.

"Get out of my way, Elsie!"

"Why? So you can tell that old lady to watch out — horrible, evil, wicked Elsie is coming?"

"Don't you dare hurt her."

"How will you stop me?"

I pushed her so hard my hands went right through her, and I fell on my face.

Elsie laughed. "When will you ever learn, Annie?"

I scrambled to my feet, but she'd disappeared. Afraid

of what she might do, I ran up three flights of stairs to warn Mrs. Jameson. By the time I reached the infirmary, I was so out of breath I could hardly talk.

Nurse Ryan frowned at me. "What brings you back again?"

"Please, just let me see Mrs. Jameson. I won't disturb her, I promise."

She fidgeted with the papers on her desk. "She's taken a turn for the worse, Annie. It's pneumonia. She—"

"Please," I begged. "Please. I promise I won't stay long. I just want to see her."

"One noise, and out you go. Do you understand?"

"Yes, ma'am."

I followed Nurse Ryan past the rows of beds where the others slept and sighed and dreamed. Someone had put a curtain around Mrs. Jameson's bed. In the glow of a lamp behind it, I made out the figure of a nurse sitting beside the bed.

I tiptoed closer and looked down at my friend. Her eyes were closed, and her breathing was loud and raspy. Her face was almost as white as the sheet on her bed. I touched her hand gently, and she opened her eyes.

"Annie," she whispered. "What's wrong? Has Elsie—"

The nurse seated beside her leaned over Mrs. Jameson. "Is this girl bothering you? I'll send her away if you wish."

"Oh, no, don't send Annie away. She's very dear to me." Mrs. Jameson's hand closed on mine as if to keep me by her side. "Could you please leave us for a while? We have important matters to discuss."

The nurse looked at me uncertainly. It was clear she didn't want to leave me alone with her patient.

"Please," Mrs. Jameson repeated. "Just a few minutes?"

The nurse rose to her feet. "I'll be at the desk with Nurse Ryan," she said. "If you need us, ring the bell beside your bed."

When she was gone, I gave Mrs. Jameson a sip of water. "Nurse Ryan says you have pneumonia, but you'll be better soon, won't you?"

"I hope so. We have many more Pickwickian adventures to share, you and I." She sighed. "And Elsie is still with us."

"She's very angry with you. I'm scared she might try to hurt you again."

"Do you know that Elsie visits me sometimes late at night when she thinks I'm asleep? If she means to harm me, she'd have done so by now."

"Elsie never said a word about it," I said. "Why does she come? What does she want?"

"I'm not sure. She sits by me, where you are now, and watches me. I keep my eyes shut and pretend to be asleep.

Sometimes she talks, but she keeps her voice so low I can't hear more than a word or two of what she says."

She paused to take another drink. "She sounds sad, not angry or hateful. It's as if there's another Elsie hiding inside the one we see. That's the Elsie you must find, Annie."

"Just before I came to see you, Elsie told me she has a lot to be sad about. As you said, she didn't sound like herself at all. It was so strange."

"What did she tell you?"

I took a deep breath. "Well, she doesn't like being dead. She knows I'll never really be her friend. But most of all, she's sad because her mother's dead. Then she got really mad and disappeared. I was scared she'd come up here and push you out of bed."

"In my younger days, I helped two or three restless spirits reunite with their deceased loved ones. Perhaps when I recover my strength . . ." Mrs. Jameson's eyes drooped. "I'm sorry, Annie, I must rest. I hope we can talk more tomorrow."

I leaned over Mrs. Jameson and kissed her. "I'll be here."

"In the meantime, remember to find Elsie's hidden self. The longer she stays here, the more wicked and dangerous she'll become."

She patted my cheek and closed her eyes. I stood beside

her and watched her fall into a deep sleep. Her breathing was fast and shallow, but she looked peaceful. "Please get well soon," I whispered.

On silent feet, Nurse Ryan came up behind me and touched my shoulder. "Say good night, Annie."

"Good night," I said softly.

At the door, I asked Nurse Ryan if I could come back tomorrow.

"We'll see." She took her seat and the other nurse returned to her vigil at Mrs. Jameson's bedside.

I met Elsie on the stairs. "She's going to die, Annie. You must know that," she said.

I ran past her. "I'm not listening to you."

Behind me, Elsie's laughter echoed in the stairwell.

TWENTY-FOUR

LATE THAT NIGHT, I woke up shivering with cold. My blanket lay on the floor. Elsie was gone. She'd left the window wide open, as if she planned to freeze me to death.

I got up to close the window and saw her dancing on the lawn. The rags of her dress fluttered, and her hair whipped around her face. The moon lit her brightly, but she cast no shadow.

Suddenly she turned to the window as if she'd sensed I was watching. "Annie," she sang, "come out to play, the moon doth shine as bright as day."

I leaned out the window. "Go away. We aren't friends anymore. Remember?"

"Come with a whoop, come with a call," she sang. "Come with a good will or not at all."

I wanted to slam the window shut and get back into bed, but what good would that do? There was no way to lock Elsie out. If I didn't go to her, she'd come to me and sing nursery rhymes all night.

She spun in circles. "You find milk and I'll find flour, and we'll have pudding in half an hour."

I watched her whirl across the grass, her arms spread, lifting into the air like a bird and swooping down to earth again. What if she wanted to say goodbye and disappear forever?

With that hope in mind, I pulled on my robe and slippers and climbed out my window. The wind felt more like winter than spring, and the grass was damp with rain from yesterday. In places, water squelched under my feet, and my slippers were soon soaked.

Elsie waited beside the pond. All her teeth were gone now. Her hair was matted with dirt. Her dress hung from her in filthy tatters. Her eyes had sunk farther into her skull, and her skin was mottled like the blotches on dead trees.

"What do you want?"

Elsie twisted a strand of hair around her finger. I was shocked to see it fall from her hand to the ground. It lay in the grass like a coil of fine-spun string. We both looked at it, but neither of us picked it up.

"Something's happening to me," Elsie said. "My hair, my teeth, my skin. I don't belong here anymore, but I don't know where I'm supposed to go. The old lady said she can help me. Do you believe her?"

"Yes."

We faced each other, Elsie and I, alone in the moonlight. She tipped her head back and looked at the stars. The Milky Way, the Big Dipper, Cassiopeia's Chair, Orion the Hunter, sprawled across the blackness. They'd been there forever, those constellations, longer than they'd had names. Long before we were born, they'd been there, and long after we died, they'd be there.

Elsie continued to stare at the sky. "Do you trust her?"

"Yes."

"What if she sends me back to my coffin to lie in the dark forever? Maybe she'll cut my head off and stuff my mouth with garlic. Maybe she'll drive a stake through my heart. Maybe she'll burn me to ashes."

"Mrs. Jameson wouldn't do any of those things. You're not a vampire or a revenant."

"She might think I am. The way you blab about me and how awful I am." Imitating what she thought I sounded like, she whined, "Oh, see what Elsie made me do. It wasn't me, it was Elsie, horrible Elsie, evil Elsie, wicked Elsie."

The sad Elsie was gone, and the angry Elsie was back. Spying a garden she'd missed, she ran about snatching the flower heads off their stems and scattering them in the grass.

I ran after her, trying to stop her, but when I grabbed her, she wasn't there — she was somewhere else, laughing at me. Frantic, desperate, she ran about, yanking off the flower heads as if it was her last chance to destroy them.

Suddenly Elsie froze and stared over my shoulder as if she saw something behind me. Slowly, I turned my head to look. A dim light floated across the lawn toward us, wobbling a bit as it came. One of the night nurses must have seen me and was coming to fetch me. What trouble I'd be in after she reported me to Dr. Benson.

"It's that crazy old lady," Elsie whispered. "She's coming to get me."

"It can't be Mrs. Jameson," I whispered back. "Her hip's broken, she has pneumonia — she can't get out of bed."

"Don't you see her? She's right there, plain as day."

I looked where Elsie pointed, but all I saw was the glow from the nurse's lantern.

Elsie ducked behind me and grasped me around my

waist. She held me so tightly I could scarcely breathe. I struggled to get away, sure she meant to suffocate me, but her grip was like death itself, cold and hard and merciless.

"What do you want, old lady?" Elsie shouted.

I heard no answer, but Elsie said, "I don't need your help. I have my friend Annie and I won't leave her!"

A breeze came up then, bringing with it the smell of lilacs. The light came closer and a hand touched my face. Slowly Mrs. Jameson began to take shape as if she'd been drawn faintly on tracing paper.

"What are you doing outside in the cold?" I cried. "I don't understand. You should be in bed."

"It's all right, Annie," she said. "I've come to take Elsie home."

"Don't believe her! She's here to get even with me!" Elsie let me go and climbed a tree. Like a wild animal, she crouched near the top and glared down through her tangle of hair. "You hate me because I pushed you down the stairs!"

"No, Elsie, I don't hate you. I simply want to help you."

"Ha," Elsie shouted. "I don't trust you one bit. You'll take me to the cemetery and put me in my coffin. You'll drive a stake through my heart to make me stay there!"

"Please come down and talk to me," Mrs. Jameson begged. "I can't climb up there, Elsie."

"Talk to me from where you are. I can hear you just fine, old lady."

"Come down, Elsie." Mrs. Jameson stretched out her hand. "Please listen to me."

Elsie stayed where she was. "Why should I do what you say?"

"Because I can take you to your mother."

"Liar. You don't know my mother. You don't know where she is." Elsie gripped the branch she sat on and stared down at Mrs, Jameson. "If my mother loved me, she'd come for me herself."

"She doesn't know the way. You must go to her. And I can show you the way."

"I don't believe you." Elsie yanked a pinecone from a branch and threw it at Mrs. Jameson. When it had no effect, she hurled another. Soon the air was full of pinecones. Some hit me, but none touched Mrs. Jameson.

"I don't have much time," Mrs. Jameson said, "and neither do you. If you don't come down soon, I'll be forced to leave without you. Once I'm gone, you'll be stranded here for a long time. Believe me, you'll be very unhappy."

"Then go, old lady, go, and leave me be! I'm staying where I am. Even if Annie won't help me, I'm not leaving until I get even with Rosie and the others."

"Elsie," I called, "please do what Mrs. Jameson says. You can trust her. She'd never lie to you."

"Ha. As if I believe a word that comes out of your lying mouth, Annie Browne. I have a mind to stay here and torment you for the rest of your life."

"That's enough, Elsie." Mrs. Jameson went to the foot of the tree. "It would break your mother's heart to see you behaving like this."

"She doesn't care about me, she never did."

"Why do you say that?"

"If she loved me, she wouldn't have died. She would've stayed with me and taken care of me."

"Nonsense." Mrs. Jameson gazed at Elsie. "Your mother didn't want to die."

Elsie began to cry. "I don't know what to do," she wailed. "I don't know where to go!"

I climbed up into the tree. She kicked my face with her bare feet, but I didn't feel anything but cold.

"Go away, Annie."

"No, not until you do what Mrs. Jameson tells you."

She climbed higher. A branch snagged her hair, and strands of it floated away on a breeze. In the bright light, I saw she'd begun to lose her edges.

"You're disappearing," I whispered.

"What does that mean?" Elsie asked.

From the ground, Mrs. Jameson answered. "It means you'll be stranded here for hundreds of years if you don't come with me now. No one will see you, no one will you hear you. You'll be all alone. An angry spirit doomed to harm the living but not to enjoy doing it. You'll be miserable."

"Maybe I won't be miserable," Elsie said. "Maybe I'll like it." Her voice shook as she spoke, and I knew she was terrified.

"Listen to what she says," I begged. "Believe her. Go with her."

Elsie looked at me and then down at Mrs. Jameson. Her grip on the branch loosened. "You better be telling the truth, old lady."

Mrs. Jameson held out her arms. "I swear to you, Elsie, you'll soon be with your mother."

Slowly Elsie let go and floated to earth. Mrs. Jameson took her hand. "How will she know me? I was just a baby when she died."

"Don't worry." Mrs. Jameson squeezed Elsie's hand. "Mothers always know their children."

Elsie frowned and smoothed her ragged dress. She touched her strands of tangled hair. "I look horrible."

"You'll look beautiful to your mother."

While they talked, my heart swelled with grief. To lose Elsie it seemed I had to lose Mrs. Jameson, too. I hadn't expected that.

"What about me?" I cried to Mrs. Jameson. "What will I do without you?"

"Oh, Annie, my dear, dear Annie. Soon you'll be home with your mother and father. You won't need me then."

Elsie scowled at me. "She's *my* friend now. Not yours."

Mrs. Jameson sighed. "Oh, Elsie, I'm Annie's friend, too. You must leave those feelings behind." She gripped Elsie's hand. "Say goodbye to Annie. We must go now."

"Well, goodbye," Elsie muttered.

I reached for Mrs. Jameson and tried to keep her for a moment but she and Elsie were both fading into the mist and shadows. There was nothing solid to hold.

"Farewell, my dear," Mrs. Jameson whispered. "I've enjoyed the time we spent together."

As the two of them disappeared into the night, three deer came to the edge of the pond and drank. A muskrat swam into sight, its slick head above the water. Overhead, the constellations kept their vigil.

Suddenly afraid, I ran across the grass and climbed through my window. On silent feet, I tiptoed through the corridors that led to the infirmary. I had to know. I had to see for myself.

At the infirmary door, I paused. The night nurse was asleep at her desk. In their beds the old people moaned and whimpered in their sleep. Some snored, some coughed, one whispered, "Who's there? Is it you, Amelia? Have you come to take me home?"

Just as I'd feared, Mrs. Jameson's bed was empty. A bare mattress stripped of sheets and blankets waited for the next occupant.

In deep sadness, I lay on her bed and looked out the window to see what Mrs. Jameson had seen. Beyond the glass was the dark sky, a sprinkle of stars, a half moon, and the constellations in their appointed places. In the distance, the lights of Mount Pleasant glowed.

"I'll miss you so much," I whispered to the listening dark.

I lay there, thinking about Mrs. Jameson. I smelled the smells she'd smelled. I heard the sounds she'd heard. I saw the things she'd seen. It was as if part of her had stayed in Cedar Grove to comfort me.

Just as the sky began to lighten, I tiptoed away, careful not to disturb the nurse or the old people wrapped in their dreams.

My own room was empty. And silent. I got into bed and pulled the covers up. Nobody would snatch them off while I slept. Nobody would throw my things on the floor.

Nobody would hang by her knees from my curtain rod. Nobody would write on my walls.

Nobody would sing "I ain't got no body."

I closed my eyes and fell into the deepest sleep I'd had for a long time.

TWENTY-FIVE

CAME HOME from Cedar Grove in April. Forsythia blazed like yellow fire. The trees were a soft golden green with the hint of new leaves, and lawns were lush with grass. The sun shone, the sky glowed deep blue with a scattering of clouds, and people strolled along the streets, some walking dogs, others pushing baby carriages, boys on bikes, girls playing jump rope.

The normal world I'd missed so much had moved from winter to spring just as it always did, but I was a stranger, a convalescent, someone who had been in a rest home. Would anyone be my friend? Or would I take Elsie's place as the outsider?

At the corner of Portman Street, Mother told me to close my eyes. "Don't open them until I tell you to."

Mystified, I did what she said. They must have a surprise for me—perhaps the shiny new bicycle I wanted.

The car stopped, and Mother said, "Open your eyes, Annie."

On our front porch, my classmates let out a cheer and held up signs welcoming me home in big red letters. Miss Harrison presented me with a bouquet of roses and hugged me. "We're so glad to see you, Annie!"

The next minute, my friends surrounded me. Everyone talked at once. They'd missed me. Had I missed them? Would I be in school on Monday? They gave me welcome-home cards they'd made in class. They hugged me. They complimented me on my dress. They admired my new patent-leather shoes. They loved the lavender ribbon in my hair.

Jane stuck by my side and clung to my hand as if I might disappear at any moment. Lucy and Eunice told me stories about school and made me laugh.

Only Rosie hung back, not quite meeting my eyes. She was thinner than I remembered. Her face was pale, and her eyes were ringed with dark circles. Her hair had lost its brightness. Worst of all, the spark that had made her our leader had disappeared.

Jane noticed me looking at Rosie. Coming closer, she

whispered, "Rosie hasn't been herself since she had the flu. She almost died, you know."

Immediately I felt guilty about the flu mask. Why had I let Elsie make me put it in Rosie's bookbag?

"Her mother and father are taking her to Hilltop Lodge for the whole summer. Dr. Hughes thinks the fresh mountain air will improve her health. She'll ride ponies and swim in the lake and play tennis. Doesn't that sound grand?"

I glanced at Rosie, still standing alone on the edge of the group. This time she looked straight at me, but she didn't smile or wave.

Without noticing Rosie, Mother walked between us. "The cake and ice cream are ready to serve, Annie. Would you like to help me?"

I followed Mother to the table she'd set up on the porch, and the girls gathered around. While Mother cut the cake, I poured glasses of punch and Miss Harrison scooped ice cream.

Rosie was the last in line. After Miss Harrison topped her slice of cake with ice cream, Rosie lingered a moment.

"I need to talk to you, Annie," she asked. "May I stop at your house on my way home from school?" Even her voice was different — flat and dull, barely louder than a whisper.

"If it's about the flu mask in your bookbag —"

"No, no. Not that. I know what happened. It's about something else altogether."

She walked through the crowd and sat on the porch steps, where she ate her cake and ice cream alone.

When everyone had finished eating, Miss Harrison called, "It's time to return to school, girls. Please thank Mrs. Browne for the delicious refreshments."

The girls moaned and groaned and begged to stay longer, but she reminded them this was a special treat for me and they mustn't tire me out. "Remember, you'll see Annie on Monday."

When they were gone, Mother noticed the yawns I tried to stifle. "You look like you need a nice rest, Annie. Why don't you go to your room and lie down for a while?"

I climbed the stairs slowly and hesitated in the doorway. My bed waited, its pillows fluffed. My books stood in straight rows on shelves. Drawing supplies lay neatly on my desk. The scent of spring drifted through the open window and stirred the curtains.

A cloud moved across the sun and darkened my room. The corners filled with shadows. Frightened, I drew back. Suppose Elsie had escaped from her grave again? Suppose she waited for me in the closet or under my bed? She might appear at any moment, swinging upside down from my curtain rod or sitting in my rocking chair, gloating. She might pick up a jar of poster paint and hurl it at the wall. Mother would think I did it, and she'd send me back to Cedar Grove, and everything would start all over again.

Suddenly Mother was beside me, her arm around my shoulders. "Is everything all right, Annie?"

I turned and clung to her as if I were three years old. "Am I really home to stay?"

Her arms tightened around me. "Yes, of course you are."

"And you'll never send me away again, no matter how bad I am?"

"Oh, darling, we didn't send you away to punish you. The concussion was worse than Dr. Hughes originally thought. He feared a swelling in your brain was causing your strange behavior. We sent you to Cedar Grove so you could get the rest and recuperation you needed."

She drew back and smiled down at me. "And just look at you. Your cheeks are pink with health, and you're yourself again. Our Annie, home to stay."

I leaned against her, breathing in the familiar lilac scent of her face powder, and knew I was safe.

Mother smoothed my hair and kissed me. "You can't imagine how empty this house has been without you."

I took off my shoes and lay on my bed. Mother covered me with a light blanket and closed the curtains. Kissing me once again, she went downstairs.

Later that afternoon, Mother shook my shoulder gently. "Wake up, Annie," she said. "Rosie is here."

Rosie sat on the parlor sofa, waiting for me. "I'm glad to see you, Annie. I missed you."

"I missed you, too."

Rosie turned her head and coughed.

"Are you all right?" I asked her.

"I'm not over the flu yet," she told me. "My mother is taking me to the mountains this summer. Dr. Hughes believes fresh air is what I need to get my strength back."

"Jane told me. She says there'll be ponies and tennis and swimming. It sounds wonderful."

Mother appeared with a tray and two glasses of lemonade. "Would you like to sit on the porch? It's a lovely day."

We followed her outside and sat side by side on the swing. I knew Mother was worried about Rosie, and I was glad she'd thought to bring us something to drink.

After Mother went back inside, Rosie said, "I didn't come here to talk about Hilltop Lodge."

Something about her voice and the look in her eyes made me nervous. "What do you want to talk about, then?"

I waited for her to go on, but she gazed silently across the lawn, beyond the tallest trees to the sky darkening now and then with passing clouds. She sat with her arms folded tightly across her chest, as if she were holding herself together. Tiny threads of blue veins were visible under the skin of her temples.

Although I'd never known Rosie O'Malley to be afraid of anything, she was definitely scared. "Tell me, Rosie," I begged. "What's frightening you?"

Without looking at me, Rosie told me. "While I was sick I had terrible dreams — not nightmares, much worse than nightmares. Dr. Hughes said they were hallucinations brought on by my fever. But I think they were real. She really was in my room, Annie. Every night, every single night, she sat on my bed and watched me. She was waiting for me to die. She knew I would. I was too sick to live much longer."

"Who?" I asked. "Who was sitting on your bed?" I waited for her to tell me, but I knew the answer already.

"You know," Rosie said. "You saw her, too."

Before I could say *Elsie,* Rosie pressed a thin, cold finger against my mouth. "Don't say her name. Don't ever say her name!"

"Why not?"

Rosie stared past me as if she saw something stir in the

shadows under the fir tree. "She might think you're calling her."

I peered into the shadows too. I saw nothing but a slight movement in the branches. The wind, I told myself, just the wind passing through. Not her, not her. But how many times had I said her name after she'd gone away? If Rosie was right . . . *No, don't think about it,* I told myself. *She's gone, gone, gone. Forever gone.*

Rosie spoke so softly I had to lean close to hear her. "She told me she made you put the flu mask in my bookbag. She said *she* gave me the flu because I stole her mask and she caught the flu and died. I had to pay for her life with mine unless I became her friend. I told her I'd rather die. She said it made no difference. Alive or dead, I'd never get away from her."

I stared at Rosie in amazement. "She told me the same thing. We'd be friends forever, just her and me, nobody else. She wanted me to help her pay back her enemies, starting with you."

Rosie seized my hands. "Oh, Annie, what will she do to us?"

I squeezed Rosie's cold hands. "She can't do anything to you or me or anyone else. She's gone forever."

"How do you know that?"

"I saw her go." While Rosie huddled beside me in the

swing, I told her about my last night with Elsie. "She left peacefully. She won't come back."

Rosie sighed deeply. We sat side by side, gently rocking the swing back and forth, back and forth. The only sound was the creak of the ropes. The sun was low now, and the shadows on the lawn were darker and longer.

⁂

On the other side of town, evening shadows crept across Forest Heights Cemetery. A solitary crow perched on the outstretched hand of a stone angel. The wind blew, and the shadows shifted. Slowly the crow lifted its wings and flew away into the dark sky.

COUNTING CROWS

One Crow for sorrow,
Two Crows for mirth;
Three Crows for a wedding,
Four Crows for a birth;
Five Crows for silver,
Six Crows for gold;
Seven Crows for a secret, not to be told;
Eight Crows for heaven,
Nine Crows for hell;
And ten Crows for the devil's own self.

—Counting Rhyme (from *The Folklore of Birds,*
   by Laura C. Martin, 1993)

AFTERWORD

One of my inspirations for this novel is a story my mother told me. In the fall of 1918, when she was twelve years old, the Spanish Influenza came to America. Before the flu ran its course in the spring of 1919, more than thirty million people had died worldwide. People likened the flu to the bubonic plague. Some thought the world's entire population would be wiped out.

In Boston, New York, and Philadelphia, people died by the thousands. There was no cure. Coffins were in short supply. Bodies were stacked in morgues waiting for burial. Streets were clogged with horse-drawn hearses. Funeral bells rang all day. Schools closed, department stores closed, theaters closed. It was unlawful to spit in the street. Handkerchiefs were required. Although flu masks did not prevent the flu's transmission, many people wore them anyway.

When World War I ended on November 11, 1918, soldiers and sailors brought an even more virulent strain of flu home with them.

My mother and her friends lived in Baltimore. That fall, they walked past many houses with black funeral wreaths on their doors. A wreath announced an occupant's death. At that time, most families kept their dead at home for a few days before they were taken away for the funeral and burial. The coffin and its occupant were on display in the parlor. Friends and relatives visited to express their condolences. The family provided refreshments.

One of my mother's friends came up with the brilliant idea of posing as acquaintances of the dead, visiting the home to express sorrow, and then partaking of the refreshments. Free cake. Free candy. Free punch. Although my mother was afraid of seeing a dead person, she went along with her friends and ate her share of sweets.

Then came the day the girls looked into a coffin and were horrified to see one of their classmates. They hadn't known she'd died. That was the end of the visitations and the free sweets.

In 1919, my mother herself came down with the Spanish Influenza. She became ill on a streetcar ride with her mother and father. By the time she got home, she had a high fever. She spent several weeks in bed, and when she recovered, she was thin and weak, too tired to do anything. To build up her strength, her parents took her to Pen Mar, a resort near the Maryland–Pennsylvania border, where she spent the summer convalescing. By August, she'd regained her energy and strength, and came home eager to see her friends.

Turn the page for a sneak peek of
The Girl in the Locked Room
by Mary Downing Hahn!

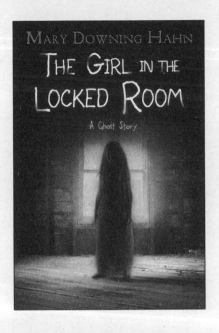

When Jules's family moves into an old, abandoned house, she feels a sense of foreboding—especially when she sees a pale face in an upstairs window. As frightened as she is, she can't stop wondering about the eerie presence on the top floor, in a room with a locked door. Could it be someone who lived in the house a century earlier?

The Girl

The girl is alone in the locked room. At first, she writes the day of the week, the month, and the year on a wall. She means to keep a record of her time in the room, but after a while she begins skipping a day or several days. Soon, days, months, and years become a meaningless jumble. She forgets her birthday. And then her name.

But what does it matter? No one comes to visit, no one asks her name, no one asks how old she is.

At first the room seems large, but soon it shrinks—or seems to. It becomes a prison. The key disappeared long ago. No matter—she's afraid to leave. They're waiting for her to open the door. She feels their presence, faint in the daytime but solid and loud at night. Their boots storm up the steps. They hammer on the door. They yell for her to come out.

But how can she? The door is locked from the outside. Even if she wanted to, she could not obey their commands. She huddles in the shadows, her eyes closed, her fingers in her ears, and waits for them to leave.

The trouble is, they always come back. Not every night, but often enough that she always waits to hear their horses gallop toward the house, to hear their boots on the stairs, to hear their fists on her door.

She used to know who they were and why they came, but now she knows only that they are bad men who will hurt her if they find her. They say they won't, but she doesn't believe them.

So she huddles in the wardrobe, under a pile of old dresses, and doesn't move until she hears their horses gallop away.

Every morning, the girl looks at a date written on the wall—June 1, 1889. She doesn't remember why she wrote the date or what happened that day. Indeed, she isn't even sure she wrote it. Maybe someone else, some other girl, was here once. Maybe that girl wrote the date.

Someone, perhaps that other girl, certainly not herself, drew pictures on the wall. They tell a story, a terrible story. The story frightens her. It makes her cry sometimes.

In a strange way, she knows the story is true, the story is about her. Not the girl she is now, but perhaps the girl she used to be before they locked her in this room.

But who was that girl? A girl should remember her own name, if nothing else. Why is her brain so fuzzy?

Near the end of the picture story, men on horses gallop to the house. They must be the ones who come to her door at night. Did they draw the pictures to scare her?

There are other paintings in the room, real paintings, beautiful paintings. A few hang on the walls, but most lean against the wall. The same people are in most of them. A pretty woman, a little girl with yellow hair, a bearded man —a family. She pretends she's the little girl. The woman is her mother. The man is her father.

She must have had a mother and a father once. Doesn't everyone?

She talks to them, and she talks for them. They have long, made-up conversations that she never remembers for more than a day.

If only she could bring them to life. They look so real. Why can't they step out of the paintings and keep her company?

✦

Years pass. The girl stops looking at the drawings on the wall. She wearies of the people in the paintings. What good are they to her? They're just faces on canvas. Flat. They cannot see her or hear her. They cannot talk to her. They cannot help her. They are useless.

She turns their faces to the wall. She forgets they are there.

✦

Seasons follow each other round and round like clockwork figures. Leaves fall, snow falls, rain falls. Flowers bloom, flowers wilt, flowers die. Snow falls again. And again. And again.

Birds nest under the eaves and sometimes find their way into the room. Trees grow taller. Their branches spread. Young trees surround the house. They push against its walls. In the summer, their leaves press against the only window and block the sunlight. The room is a dim green cave.

Brambles and vines climb the stone walls. Their roots burrow into cracks and crevices, and they cling tight. Tendrils manage to find their way inside. Every year, their leaves fall on the floor of her room.

Gradually the house blends into the woods, and people forget it's there.

The girl stays in the locked room and waits. She no longer knows who or what she is waiting for. Something, someone . . .

She is lonelier than you can imagine.

2

The Girl

One morning, the girl hears loud noises from somewhere outside. It sounds as if an army has invaded the woods, bent on attacking and destroying everything in its path.

Confused and frightened, the girl hides in her nest. Buried completely under the rags of dresses, she hears sounds she can't identify, louder even than thunder. They come closer. The trees surrounding the house crash to the ground. Sunlight pours through the window. She squints and shields her eyes with her hand.

Outside, near the house, men shout. Who are they? Where have they come from? Why are they here? Have they come for her?

She smells smoke. They must be burning something.

Suppose the fire spreads to the house? She trembles. She'll have no place to hide.

Men enter the house. They tramp about downstairs. They speak in loud voices. They come to the second floor and then the third. Their footsteps stop at her door. The doorknob turns, but without the key, the men can't come in.

The girl burrows deeper into the rags. She doesn't think they're the ones who come on horseback at night. They don't pound on the door or shout at her, but she doesn't want them to know she's here — just in case. So she remains absolutely still.

Just outside her door, she hears a man say, "This is the only room in the house that's locked. Should we bust it open and take a look?"

The girl cringes in her hiding place. She's sure the men will find her.

"Nah," says another. "Nothing in there but trash and broken stuff."

The men shuffle past the door and go downstairs, laughing about something as they go.

When she's sure they won't come back, she tiptoes to the window and looks out. A huge yellow machine with long, jointed arms lifts and lowers, lifts and lowers, scooping up things from one place and dumping them somewhere else. Its jaws have sharp teeth.

Not far from the yellow machine are red machines with scrapers attached to their fronts. They push mounds of grassy earth into piles of red clay. Other machines have rollers that flatten everything, even hills.

She's never seen anything like these contraptions. They're bigger than steam locomotives and much scarier. Trains stay on tracks; they can't hurt you if you stay off the tracks. But these machines can go anywhere. Nothing is safe from them.

While they work, the machines roar and snort and make beeping sounds. They puff clouds of smoke into the air. The girl covers her ears, but she can still hear the noise they make.

A flash of movement catches her eye. A rabbit runs across the muddy ground. She holds her breath and prays the machines won't kill him. He disappears behind a pile of tree stumps, and she lets out her breath in a long sigh.

But where will the rabbit live? The fields have been destroyed, the woods chopped down. The men and their machines are everywhere. She wishes she could go outside and bring the rabbit to her room.

✦

Day after day, the girl watches the wreckage spread. The men and their machines cut down more trees and destroy barns and sheds. They haul furniture from the house. Sofas and chairs, their velvet upholstery stained, faded, and torn. Stuffing hangs out of holes. She sees a bed missing a leg, a bureau without drawers, a large broken mirror, fancy tables with cracked marble tops.

Did she once sit on that sofa, curl up in those chairs, sleep in that bed, look at herself in that mirror? Now everything is ruined. It's of no use to her or anyone else.

The men pile up the broken furniture and set fire to it. The smoke drifts up to her window and stings her eyes. She feels as if she's watching her life turn to ashes along with the sofas and chairs.

The men don't stop with the furniture. They burn tree stumps, carts, wagons, fences, and stacks of boards. The fire smolders for days. After dark, the embers glow and the night wind teases flickers of flames from charred wood. The smell of smoke poisons the air.

When nothing's left to burn, the men turn the fields to mud and plow roads through them. On the flat land below her window, they dig deep square holes. Their nightmare machines destroy everything in their way. Her world disappears before her eyes.

✦

Then comes a quiet time. Machines still shake the ground, but they're down on the flat land now, hard at work building houses. The girl's home is empty again. Peaceful. She spends most of her time at the window, watching and listening, enjoying the summer breeze and the smell of honeysuckle.

She keeps her eyes focused on the distant mountains, blue and serene against the sky. She doesn't look at the fields and meadows destroyed by the machines.

One afternoon she dreams of a picnic by a stream. She's sitting under a tree with a man and a woman. She's had this dream many times. But it always ends before she's ready. She wakes up reaching for the man and woman, but it's too late. They're gone, and she's alone in the locked room.

Read more ghost stories from
MARY DOWNING HAHN: